SNARE

Other books by Gwen Moffat:

Hard Road West
Over the Sea to Death
Miss Pink at the End of the World
Space Below My Feet

GWEN MOFFAT

SNARE

St. Martin's Press
New York

SNARE. Copyright © 1987 by Gwen Moffat. All rights reserved.
Printed in the United States of America. No part of this book may
be used or reproduced in any manner whatsoever without written
permission except in the case of brief quotations embodied in
critical articles or reviews. For information, address St. Martin's
Press, 175 Fifth Avenue, New York, N.Y. 10010.

Library of Congress Cataloging-in-Publication Data

Moffat, Gwen.
    Snare : a Miss Pink mystery.

    I. Title.
PR6063.04S6 1988   823'.914   88-15865
ISBN 0-312-02284-0

First published in Great Britain by Macmillan London Limited.

First U.S. Edition

10 9 8 7 6 5 4 3 2 1

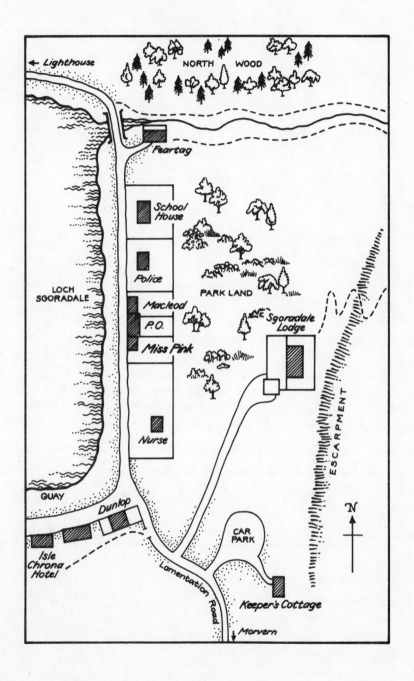

← *Lighthouse*

NORTH WOOD

Feartag

School House

Police

LOCH SGORADALE

Macleod

P.O.

Miss Pink

PARK LAND

Sgoradale Lodge

Nurse

ESCARPMENT

QUAY

Dunlop

Isle Chrona Hotel

CAR PARK

Lamentation Road

Keeper's Cottage

↓ *Morvern*

N
↑

Chapter 1

Ivar Campbell was dangerous. He wasn't violent, he wasn't in a bad mood; it was just that the wild geese were flying south and they had this effect on him. He was tinder waiting for a spark, a ticking bomb, a man born out of his time.

He came out of the Post Office and paused as he caught the sound of the geese passing over. Late September in the far north of Scotland and the air was warm enough for high summer. Hens crooned in the dust, eider duck talked at the edge of the loch, a buzzard mewed above the North Wood. Campbell stood immobile, his eyes shadowed by the peak of his cap, listening and watching.

All boys dream, but Campbell's dreams had stayed with him. Before marriage he had considered becoming a mercenary, a detective, a spy. He read a great deal and all his heroes had blended to form the image of a tall, thin, loping man with restless eyes and a drooping moustache: a copy of himself.

He had left his Glasgow comprehensive school at sixteen to work in a garage, but although he was a competent mechanic he found the job stultifying. He lived for his books in the evenings, for camping trips at weekends when he could indulge the fantasy of a man on the run, a scenario varied only by the alternative: the killer on the prowl.

Then he met Debbie, a nursing auxiliary: a country girl disenchanted with urban life, who wanted only to return to the Highlands and raise a family. They married and Campbell threw up his job and bought an old van in which they lived for a summer, drifting up the west coast until Debbie discovered she was pregnant. They were then at Sgoradale, a crofting township at the end of a road.

Debbie found work as a housemaid to Lady MacKay at Sgoradale Lodge, and they moved into the old keeper's cottage in the woods. Over the next ten years Campbell established himself in the community as an odd-job man. The boredom threshold was higher on this wild coast, but it was still there. Fishing and tree-felling, draining and fencing occupied his hands but not his mind. Another child followed the first and he discovered that family responsibilities were a world away from that free-ranging life which had been the dream before he met Debbie.

He returned to reading, switching now from fiction to true-life accounts of adventure, espionage, crime. Debbie accepted his absorption as easily as she accepted his ability to understand and use long words. Only recently, when the Russians hit the headlines and Campbell started to tell lies, did she start to wonder if all that reading was something more than a harmless hobby.

Soviet trawlers had been using the little port of Ullapool for years, but suddenly an enterprising reporter realised that no one kept surveillance on the landing parties. No one counted them back. The scandal was a nine-day wonder and, further up the coast, Campbell's expertise was acknowledged. His fantasies were private, but everyone knew he was the authority on espionage. His opinion was sought, he became the arbitrator in the inevitable bar-room arguments. He swelled and bloomed – and started to drop hints of a dark and secret life before he came to Sgoradale. He wished passionately that a Russian trawler would put into the loch but he knew it wouldn't happen now, at the end of the season, when any foreigner would be as conspicuous as a Siberian bear.

And yet there was a stranger in Sgoradale, which was why he lingered outside the Post Office after the geese had gone. His gaze slid over the grey water, past the cormorant that surfaced off the steps where his boat was moored, to come to rest on the figure at the head of those steps, its hands to its temples in the unmistakable stance of one using binoculars. Campbell, the observer, was being observed.

He looked away quickly, seaward. With peripheral vision he caught a movement and smiled thinly. She, too, had turned towards the mouth of the loch. I've got her now, he thought; she has to pass me to get away. He had been stalking her for two days, looking for a chance to engage her in conversation and discover what kind of story she would give him to explain her presence in the far north of Scotland at the back-end of the year. She had avoided him, not once but twice. Once could have been arrogance – she was old, but she was a lady – but twice was suspect. And why should Rose Millar, the post-mistress, deflect his questions concerning the visitor? That had peculiar significance given that Rose was a government servant. Campbell climbed into his van and drove to the quay.

She was still at the top of the steps. He pulled up more sharply than he'd intended and the tools in the back shifted with a clatter. She regarded him from behind thick spectacles with green frames: a large solid lady with trim grey hair, wearing tweeds and clumpy shoes with huge serrated tongues. The binoculars were Zeiss. Campbell nodded curtly, opened the back of the van and reached in for a petrol can, remembering to heft it as if it were full.

At the top of the steps he paused and surveyed the sky.

'Is the weather going to break?' she asked pleasantly.

'It won't break today, ma'am.' He grimaced as the courtesy slipped out. His tone hardened. 'Were you wanting to go out?' He nodded towards his boat.

'I hadn't thought of it. Is that yours: *Blue Zulu*? Why did you call it that?'

He stared at her. 'She was called that when I bought her.'

'You were not curious yourself?'

His anger flared. Questions were his job, not hers. 'So,' he said heavily, 'you're staying next to the Post Office. You'll be writing a book?'

Her eyes were steady. 'That's a possibility. Where do you stay, Mr—?'

'I use the Post Office for an address. People contact me there if they need me.'

There was a pause. 'You keep a low profile,' she observed.

'Exactly.' He was pleased that she should gauge him correctly, but he would play it cool. 'I'm not much bothered, but in my line it's always a good idea. . . . I come and go; mail drops are convenient, you know, like collecting spots?'

3

'Your line, Mr—?'

'Campbell. Ivar. I'm . . . ' The eyes shifted, ranged the water and returned to her. 'I'm a handyman,' he told her blandly. She smiled and waited. He glanced at the empty windows of the hotel at the back of the quay and lowered his voice. 'You've been listening to the talk. You shouldn't believe everything you hear. I left all that behind when I came to Sgoradale. Mind you, I'm not saying it's over; it can never be over, but I've got a wife and family to think of now. If I accept anything nowadays, it's just routine work.' His smile was smug; it was almost a leer. He saw her surprise and he giggled. 'Not contracts—' He stared at the twin discs of her spectacles, saw his own reflection and added wildly, 'There'll be time enough for contract work when the children leave home.' He gave her a fierce frown, nodded, turned on his heel and strode to the truck, swinging the can.

His old Morris crept up the quay with a slow menace that was belied by its dangling exhaust and a trail of orange baler twine protruding from an ill-fitting rear door.

Miss Pink followed thoughtfully, wondering how long he had been what Rose Millar called 'a wee strange in his ways'. It had been a short encounter and he'd been consumed by a kind of demon as if, in accosting her, he'd been conforming to an image. Well, the ice had been broken; next time he might have more confidence.

She dismissed him and sauntered along the quay observing Sgoradale with approval. From here the Post Office and its adjoining neighbours (the nearer rented by herself) were the focal point of the one street, but on either side of this short terrace were houses each standing in its own plot of land: the old schoolhouse, the police house, the nurse's bungalow. Miss Pink had been here only three days and if she hadn't met everyone she knew where they lived – at least, those who lived in the street.

On the far side of the bay that was the head of the loch, seaward of the hanging woods, was a scatter of crofts and that grim reminder of the Clearances: the sad grey stumps of ruins. On this side, at the back of the quay and inland of the fish sheds, was the Isle Chrona Hotel – a sprawling whitewashed building, all corners and extensions, with dormers, gables and a glazed verandah. The food was execrable. She had dined there once and next day had laid in a stock of tinned ravioli to serve against future emergencies.

Beyond the hotel with its garages, barns and disused stables were several cottages on a bend in the road, the approach road that was known locally as Lamentation because it had been built during the potato famine of 1846. At the other end of the so-called street the highway crossed a stone bridge above the mouth of the River Ord, then swung sharp left through the North Wood to run down the shore of the loch and end at the lighthouse on Fair Point.

Miss Pink's attention returned to the foregound, noting that the largest house in the village was the only one to guard its privacy. Sgoradale Lodge was scarcely visible from sea level; only the upper slates of its roofs and the top of a crenellated tower showed above magnificent trees. Behind and above the lodge loomed an escarpment of rock below which the township nestled like the first colony on a strange continent.

The simile of stalwart pioneers did not extend to the inhabitants, at least not to sweet, fat Alec Millar from the Post Office, now coming carefully along the stone flags of the quay. Alec was always unsure of his footing. Some years ago he had contracted meningitis and had been left with brain damage, although the only obvious signs were a childlike mentality and a tendency to convulsions. He had worked in a bank: a clever man, destined to become branch manager, according to his mother. Now he was an overgrown child with nice manners and an overwhelming passion for a miniature apricot poodle called Baby.

'A fine morning, Alec.' Miss Pink, who had been nipped by Baby, made no move to touch her.

'Great!' His eyes shone behind his pebble spectacles. 'Are you going out with Ivar?'

'Perhaps.'

He looked down the loch. 'I love going out in a boat—' Miss Pink opened her mouth, then closed it, but he'd noticed. 'They wouldn't let me come,' he told her. 'I could fall overboard. I

5

can swim but that's no good if I faint, is it? I'm too heavy for you to get me back in the boat.'

'There's a steamer that goes round the Summer Isles in the season. Go with your mother and have a picnic.'

'She wouldn't go if there wasn't a doctor on board.'

'There's no doctor within fifteen miles of Sgoradale, Alec. I'm sure your mother copes very well if you faint, doesn't she?'

'I don't know.'

She changed the subject. 'Is this your regular walk?'

'In the morning. After dinner I go the other way, past the big house. Usually I come down here later, when the bar's open. I have one beer; that takes ten minutes. I can stay longer, so long as I don't have more'n one beer. The visitors talk to me and they want to buy me drink, but I mustn't let them.'

'It's the fainting, isn't it? You could have a nasty fall. You're a big man.'

'Be thankful for small mercies,' he said cheerily, evidently echoing his mother. 'I can look after myself and I enjoy my food, and I got Baby here.'

Miss Pink and Baby exchanged wary glances. Alec said, peering, 'Who's that in your garden, miss?'

'In my garden? I can't see anyone.'

'They're gone now. Maybe it was my father. I don't see all that well.'

'But . . . it doesn't matter. We're all friends.' With which inane comment she left him and made her way home, pondering his gentle nature, forgetting the possibility of an intruder in her garden until she entered her kitchen and was astonished to find the daylight blocked. A figure was outside, its hands shading reflections from the glass, peering round the interior until it spied Miss Pink. A grin materialised like that of the Cheshire cat, a hand waved, lips moved, there were faint calls of greeting. Miss Pink made no move towards the back door but that was immaterial; her presence was known and the front door was open.

Esme Dunlop knocked superfluously as she stepped in from the street: a large, ungainly woman in her fifties in fawn trousers with a knife-edged crease, a Viyella shirt and burgundy pullover. Her expression was as ingenuous as her style. She brimmed with enthusiasm and, having encountered her several times already, Miss Pink had found herself reflecting that such relentless exuberance might prove tiresome on occasions – upon bereavement for instance, or if one were trying to do something quietly without attracting attention.

'I went round the back,' Esme was saying. 'I got no reply at the front, so I thought you must be in the garden. You've got a wilderness out there! I wasn't really surprised. I mean, Coline owns the holiday homes but who looks after them?'

Miss Pink refused to be steam-rollered. 'Gardens always look unkempt at this time of year—'

'It's the same in here—' Esme wasn't listening. Her eyes probed the corners of the living room. 'Mary MacLeod is supposed to look after this property, but look at it! If I spent a couple of hours in this room you wouldn't recognise it.'

Miss Pink had, in fact, spent an appreciable time cleaning her one reception room when she moved in. She had even polished the table.

'It's not dirty,' she said firmly.

'Well – those loose covers haven't seen the inside of a washing machine for yonks, but I was thinking in terms of a spot of polish and some elbow grease. Look at that table. . . . Is this your latest book—' Esme advanced heavily.

Miss Pink skirted a chair and placed one hand on a pile of manuscript, forestalling her visitor. 'It's not a book as yet; merely a draft.'

'That has to be typed.' It was a flat statement. 'And that's your typewriter?' Regarding the portable as if it were a museum piece, Esme gave a snicker of amazement. She said decisively, 'Look, I'll tell you what we'll do. What you want is a secretary, and here I am, with oodles of free time at my disposal. Coline's between books at this moment. I've got an electric typewriter and I'm an excellent typist. None of your two-finger pecking for me. I'll come over each morning – better still, you give me that manuscript and I'll return it to you, clean as a whistle, in three days. With all the spelling mistakes and grammar corrected: word-perfect, guaranteed. How's that?' Her beam split her face.

Miss Pink hesitated, and Esme pounced. 'I promise you, I've got nothing else to do. It'll be a pleasure. Give it to me now—' Their hands shot out simultaneously, but Miss Pink was the quicker. Esme wasn't beaten. 'Half price?' She twinkled roguishly. 'I shall adore reading it.'

Miss Pink struggled with her reactions. 'No,' she said, and knew she sounded aggressive. 'You're accustomed to Lady MacKay's methods—'

'No problem! All grist to the mill. I'm adaptable – and we're all alike: romantic and gothic, the three of us—'

'I want a man,' Miss Pink said loudly and, since she had managed to silence Esme, went on more quietly, 'I prefer working with men; their angle is different, and refreshing.'

Esme was all contrition. 'I was crowding you. You've only known me three days. And here I am, a total stranger, proposing to take more than half your work-load on my broad shoulders. Look, forget I ever proposed the arrangement, at least for the time being' – she grinned happily – 'and I'll forget the crack about a male secretary, right? I'll leave you now to get down to work, and we'll meet this evening.' She thrust past the sofa to the door and paused on the step. 'We don't dress, you know, nothing formal.' Her gaze travelled from Miss Pink's hair to her brogues. 'Tweeds would *do*,' she added doubtfully.

Miss Pink walked along the street to take morning coffee with Beatrice Swan, whom she'd met on the foreshore two days ago while watching the waders. An old lady, emerging from the Post Office (which was also the store), had crossed the road and introduced herself. Having chatted about the local wildlife, she had indicated a house she called Feartag and extended the invitation to coffee. Miss Pink, observing the old but beautifully tailored Harris tweed, the leathery skin and serene eyes, sensed a kindred spirit: another loner living out her remaining years on the fringe of the wilderness.

Feartag was at the far end of the street where the road crossed the river before turning west towards Fair Point. The house had been built just upstream of the bridge and some thirty feet above the water which, in a dry autumn, was merely a stream between boulders. It was approached by a gravel drive between lawns which were still mown. Grass had a long growing season in this climate, where the Gulf Stream lapped the shores.

Feartag was Victorian; there were sash windows downstairs but the upper storey was in the roof, its dormers whimsically fitted with casements of leaded lights. The roof was purple slate; even the porch had its own neat cap of slates, supported at each corner by knotted trunks of Scots pine. The front door was open on a passage where a bowl of sweet peas stood on an oak table. Above it, on the planked wall, was a narwhal's tusk of spiralled ivory.

Beatrice appeared in answer to the knock and, seeing Miss Pink's interest, remarked that her brother had brought home the tusk from Greenland: 'The narwhal is called the unicorn of the ocean. Isn't that lovely?'

She showed the visitor into a room that extended the width of the house. French windows opened on a terrace and Miss Pink was taken outside to admire tints in the birches opposite and the water chuckling among pink rocks below a stout fence of post and rails. There were two doors at the back of the house, one leading to the kitchen, the other open on a dim room Beatrice called the log cellar. There was a strong smell of sawn timber.

'We took a tree down,' Beatrice said. 'We must get all the logs under cover before it rains, although there's little sign of that. These autumnal days are delightful, but there's a nip in the air when you're out of the sunshine. Come inside and we'll have some coffee.'

The sitting room was homely, with white walls and old furniture that was mostly oak. The floor was parquet, the carpet oriental, its jewelled shades echoed by paisley cushions on a coral sofa. One wall was lined with book-shelves, but there was also a television set and a record player.

Beatrice came in with the coffee and they settled to small talk. Miss Pink didn't mention the brother but after he had, as it were, obtruded twice on the conversation, she wondered how long her hostess could refrain from doing so. 'We are well above flood level,' she said of the river and, acknowledging a compliment on the garden, 'We're fortunate; there's a man who comes twice a week to mow the grass and cut up dead trees and so on. We do all the light work ourselves.'

At that she looked uncomfortable and conversation dried up for a moment.

'You don't live alone?' Miss Pink's tone was light.

Beatrice was still. 'I'm alone now,' she said. 'I lost my brother two years ago.'

'I'm sorry.'

'He wasn't ill for long.' The tone was flat. 'It was cancer. He was in hospital, but he came home at the end.' She looked round the room and her lips moved in the travesty of a smile. 'Life goes on, doesn't it? Do you have any brothers or sisters?'

'I was an only child. My father died when I was young, but I was devastated when my mother died. I was in my late forties.'

'What did you do? I mean, how did you cope once you'd recovered from the shock?'

'I worked,' Miss Pink said. 'I started writing stories and articles for magazines while I looked after my mother. She had a long illness. But I wasn't alone after she died. I had, and still have, an excellent housekeeper. I've never been lonely.' There was a silence which stretched too far. 'There was always something to do,' she went on, 'even if I had to fabricate it. Unfortunately that gets more difficult with age, at the same time as the writing becomes easier. So I started to travel.'

'Did that work?'

'It worked very well. I was something of a mountaineer when I was younger and I'd always thought I would have made a good explorer. When I go abroad, I don't exactly court danger but I don't go out of my way to avoid it. And there's nothing to bring back the old joy of living so much as a good dose of fear.'

'I was the timid one,' Beatrice said. 'Robert was the explorer. He crossed Greenland by dog sledge; he was in Spitzbergen, Baffin Land, the Yukon.'

'Robert Swan!' Miss Pink was amazed. 'Of course. The polar traveller. I knew the name was familiar.'

'You must come one evening and see some of his slides. I'll

10

put on a show.' Beatrice smiled engagingly. 'He used to call me his producer. I always helped select the pictures for a new lecture, and he tried out his commentary on me. I was representative of his audience, you see. He knew how mountaineers' minds worked but he didn't understand people who stayed at home.'

'Did you always live together?'

'Since the war. I had two more brothers. One was killed in a Japanese prisoner-of-war camp in Burma, the other was a bomber pilot. He was shot down over the Ruhr. Robert went through North Africa without a scratch. Afterwards he worked for oil companies – he was a geologist – but when our parents died and we inherited, he didn't need to do that kind of work any longer, so he explored and lectured. We came here in 1950. He loved Sgoradale – for a few months at a time – and then he'd be off again to some wild corner of the world. Are you like that: unable to spend long at home?'

'I've not yet found a home,' Miss Pink confessed. 'I thought it was North Wales, then Cornwall – where I still have a house. It doesn't bother me; I'm not looking for a home. No doubt the right place will appear in due course.'

'You're good for the soul. When will you be free to come for a meal?'

'I'm dining at the lodge tonight. Is tomorrow too short notice?'

'Not at all. Everyone in Sgoradale has freezers. Tomorrow it is. Shall we say six-thirty since we're to have a slide show?'

Miss Pink made her way along the street. The tide was high, lapping close to the green turf on the other side of the road. Across the bay a boat broke away from the steps and headed down the loch, the sound of its outboard coming over the water moments after it had picked up speed. She had meant to ask her hostess about Ivar Campbell's background – what, in jargon, constituted his motivation. There had been no gossip from Beatrice Swan but, despite a conversation that had never overstepped the bounds of propriety, there had been a sense of self-exposure. Predictable, of course. There hadn't been a sign of so much as a cat. Sgoradale would be a subjective place – heaven or hell or lotus-land depending on how you looked at it. In such an environment, Esme Dunlop's gush and Campbell's shiftiness did not seem excessive. Could they be defence mechanisms mutated in a rarefied atmosphere?

Miss Pink pondered the kind of eccentricities the MacKays might exhibit. She decided on a stiff walk from Fair Head to blow her mind clear and strengthen her defences for dinner at Sgoradale Lodge.

Chapter 2

Miss Pink drove to Fair Point, left her car outside the gates of the lighthouse and started along a sheep path which meandered through heather towards a craggy knoll. From this pimple of a hill, Sgoradale appeared more than ever like an outpost of civilisation. Even its sheltering escarpment was diminished, for behind it the high ground stretched across Scotland, fretted with spires and elephantine humps of hills, with glimpses of water like shattered sapphires in the peat and, most distantly, grey ranges frosted with the first snowfall.

Sgoradale turned its back on this hinterland, facing down the loch past wooded islets to skerries that marked the open sea. The sides of the loch were steep and, near the water, they were clothed with hardwoods now patched with gold as the leaves started to turn. Beyond the mouth of the loch and across the Minch, the Hebrides appeared like a fairy land on the horizon.

Miss Pink was not deceived by the gentle beauty of the scene. She could visualise Atlantic gales driving across the loch, lacy waterfalls swollen to brown torrents, blizzards where now the lochans reflected blue sky. Strolling back to the car she passed a ruin: a gable end above a scatter of stones. She remembered the Clearances, when cottages were fired and crofters evicted (cats thrown back in the flames) to make room for commercially viable sheep. There was a smell of blood and soot and burned fur. She shuddered; elemental violence was terrible, but it lacked malice. That was a human attribute.

'We have no local crime. No doubt we lose a few fish to the pot here and there, even deer, but I've seen no evidence of it. Poaching is traditional, y'know – wasn't there a Norman king killed by a poacher? But they must follow up and kill a beast if it's been wounded. Only criminals leave a wounded beast to die

13

slowly. And poachers must not get caught; that's another crime.'

Sir Ranald MacKay grinned impishly at Miss Pink and waited for her reaction. They were in the drawing room at the lodge – a wood-panelled room ornamented with the heads of dead animals. Lamps cast pools of light downwards and the place had that dim glow characteristic of Victorian interiors. At one time this building, all slate and stone, would have been cold comfort; now it was centrally heated and a log fire burned in the basket grate. Miss Pink, chic in grey cashmere, sipped her Tio Pepe and considered her response. Sir Ranald, a large man, balding but trendy in light tweeds and a tie the colour of egg yolk, was waiting.

'No crime at all?' she ventured. 'What about drugs?'

'You mean the hard stuff? Cocaine, heroin? Not locally. In Ullapool perhaps, or Oban, but even there it would be brought in by foreigners, Scandinavians probably; Sweden was first with the permissive society. And there are always the Russians.'

'Glue sniffing?' Miss Pink suggested, her ears alert to the sound of heels on the tiled floor.

The women who entered the drawing room were in sharp contrast to each other. The first was tall and thin, with the kind of bony elegance achieved by rigid dieting. She was wearing highwaisted gaucho pants with a bolero, all in white, a black shirt and gold chains with a pendant that was one large pearl. She was a tawny blonde with a mass of loose curls to her shoulder-blades. In that dim light, it was only her poise as she greeted her guest that suggested she was over thirty. Lady MacKay's age was not public knowledge, but her string of romantic novels (notably their publication dates) proved that she'd never see forty again.

Miss Pink shook hands and turned to Flora MacKenzie, Coline MacKay's daughter, Sir Ranald's step-child. She was young, plump with the softness of puppy fat, her face delicately boned under the roundness, with large clear eyes. She had her mother's tawny hair, but straight and cut short with a heavy fringe. She looked twelve years old, innocent but rich. Only the child of wealthy parents would come down to dinner in stained cotton pants several sizes too large, worn with a bulky blouson in shimmering colours that must have cost a fortune.

'Glue sniffing?' Coline repeated, helping herself to sherry. 'Are we having that kind of party?'

Ranald said, frowning, 'Miss Pink was asking about the incidence of local crime. I told her we don't have any. Knox, the police constable, takes care of the drunks on a Saturday night, and if there's a trawler in, the hands stagger straight across the quay and fall in their bunks – if they don't fall in the water!' He chuckled heartily.

Coline sat down on a sofa. 'Nothing happens in Sgoradale,' she said. 'Except the weather, which can be very dreary, but then we're all going to Bermuda in November, thank God! The only thing one can do here in winter is write, but I can do that in the sun too.'

'Sgoradale can be lovely,' Flora said. 'Spring is gorgeous. And in summer it can be roasting hot – just like the Caribbean.'

'The Caribbean doesn't have trippers,' Ranald said darkly. He looked towards Miss Pink. 'Now that's when we have crime; it comes with the gangs, the vandals – why, this June and July we had, what' – he glanced at his wife – 'five, six cars broken into? It was a gang from Inverness.'

'It wasn't proved,' Coline reminded him. 'No one was arrested, and there were two incidents after they left.'

'How do you know they left? They weren't seen, that's all. They were probably camping on the moor and sneaked back to the car park through the woods.'

'I haven't seen a car park,' Miss Pink said.

'It's not obvious.' Ranald preened himself. 'It's a corner of the estate, in the woods just south of the village. Unfortunately, in hiding it away we made it vulnerable to thieves. There's no attendant, you see.'

'What was stolen?'

'Money. Men take their wallets with them, but women leave their bags in the car: covered, but not always locked in the boot. Although, given this gang, a locked boot wouldn't have stopped them.'

'Did they take credit cards?' Miss Pink asked, and had all their attention.

15

'That never occurred to me,' Coline said. 'Were credit cards taken, dear?'

'I don't know. Never asked. Knox would know. Not important, is it?' He regarded Miss Pink doubtfully.

'Taking only cash implies an amateur. A professional thief could get a better haul by way of credit cards – provided he acted quickly – than he could by stealing cash directly from cars.'

'They were amateurs,' Ranald protested. 'A gang of Hell's Angels working their way round the coast.'

'Was that the kind of crime you were thinking of?' Flora asked politely. 'Or were you suggesting we might be into . . . ' she sought for the correct term ' . . . capital offences?'

Coline sighed. '"Capital" means the kind of thing you could be hanged for once, sweetie. I don't think we indulge in murder and . . . high treason? Nor even espionage, despite Campbell's insistence that any of the villages on this coast could be harbouring a sleeper.'

'A sleeper?' Ranald goggled at her.

'A spy.' Flora was patient with him. 'Like the KGB, or whoever, had put someone in Sgoradale – Campbell, for instance – ten years ago, complete with a wife (who'd be working for them too) and he lived a normal life until someone decided to base nuclear submarines in the loch, and Campbell would be activated. To get the plans of the submarines, or blow them up, or pervert the crews.'

'Subvert,' Coline corrected.

Ranald blinked. 'You've got too vivid an imagination.'

'No.' Flora was cool. 'I'm just observant – like Campbell. In fact, it was he who told me about sleepers.'

'He mentioned contracts when I met him,' Miss Pink said. 'I might have thought he was talking about employment, but he took pains to emphasise the other meaning. Whether he meant he would accept a contract or thought himself the target for one escaped me.'

'What kind of contract was he talking about?' Ranald looked bewildered.

Flora said calmly, 'He'd be wanting her to think he was a hit

16

man.' He made to interrupt, but she went on, 'A hit man is hired to "take out" someone – meaning terminate, or kill, like culling stags. It's a verbal contract.'

'Good God, that's Chicago stuff! Al Capone and – and Butch Cassidy.' He rose and went to the sideboard where the drinks were. He looked back at his step-daughter. 'Campbell told you all this?'

'Where d'you spend your time? Miss Pink's been here three days and knows Campbell has – what is it, Mum – *folie de grandeur*? And you've employed him for ten years and what do you know? You block things out.'

'I know he's barmy.'

'He's harmless,' Coline said equably. 'A good workman, an unremarkable family man – well, he doesn't beat his wife. . . .' She giggled. 'Rose Millar says he's started using the Post Office as a *poste restante*.'

'He told me that,' Miss Pink said. 'How long has he been like this?'

Coline shrugged. 'Probably since he came.'

'He's getting worse,' Ranald said.

Coline sighed. 'So long as he doesn't upset Debbie.' She turned to Miss Pink. 'Local women won't work in the house,' she explained. 'They think domestic service is degrading. Our cook's on holiday and we're managing with Mary MacLeod, who looks after the holiday cottages, and Debbie Campbell. Esme Dunlop will help out when necessary – this evening, for instance. She's my secretary, but she can turn her hand to most things.'

'She called on me this morning,' Miss Pink said.

'She said so,' Ranald put in. 'Said she thought she frightened you.'

Miss Pink's jaw dropped and Flora looked at her with interest.

'She had a look at the black colt,' Ranald continued. 'She inspects his leg every day.'

'Don't you do that, sweetie?' Coline asked her daughter. 'They're your ponies.'

'I do it,' Flora said. 'Every day.'

17

'She thought he was moving a bit stiffly this afternoon,' Ranald said. 'She put a clean dressing on. Animal cut himself on some wire,' he told Miss Pink.

'Couldn't you change the dressing yourself?' Flora asked. 'Or you could have asked me.'

'She wouldn't trust me to do it.' Again he addressed himself to the guest. 'Esme's as good as a man: she keeps an eye on the horses, the cattle, even the big trees – tells me when they need pruning or a branch gets dangerous; she keeps the pool clean, supervises the servants—'

'She does *what?*' Flora was strident. Miss Pink was not surprised; Ranald did seem to be piling it on.

He gave an embarrassed cough and glanced at his wife, who said, 'We need all the help we can get – and she takes the grind out of writing as far as I'm concerned.'

'I do love accolades,' said a new voice, and Miss Pink turned to see Esme Dunlop. She wondered how long the woman had been there in the shadows.

'Good evening, Miss Pink.' She came forward, incongruous in high-necked, long-sleeved red *moiré*, very tall in her high heels. 'Sable is doing fine, Flora; you'll be able to start exercising him in a fortnight.' She turned to Coline. 'Everything's under control,' she said quietly. 'They'll be dishing up in ten minutes, OK?'

'Perfect. Help yourself to a drink.'

'Can I top up anyone?' Esme looked brightly round the room and replenished other people's glasses before pouring herself a small gin and drowning it in tonic. She sat down beside Coline and beamed. The others sipped their fresh drinks, all except Flora who, drinking nothing at all, slumped in a deep chair and regarded the fire without expression.

Esme said, 'How did you find Beatrice, Miss Pink?'

The grapevine, thought Miss Pink. Aloud she said, 'Well. Has she been ill?'

'She took her brother's death very hard.' Esme's tone was reverent. 'She retreated into herself, you know? Shunned people. We had to be quite firm with her.'

'You were,' Flora murmured as her step-father nodded

18

confirmation. 'She was very much attached to Robert,' he informed Miss Pink. 'She told you about him? Yes, well, they never married, either of them, and then – the two brothers killed in the war, the parents dying shortly afterwards – they'd been a big family and there were just the two of them left. Yes, she took his death hard.'

'He was a colourful character.' Coline smiled. 'I put him in a number of books.'

'You don't have explorers in your books,' Ranald protested. 'They're all doctors and nurses or tycoons and secretaries: dull people.'

'But with romantic souls. Robert was what all my heroes would like to be.'

'Not me.' He eased himself in his chair. 'I like my creature comforts. Eight hours on the moor is as much as I can take in dirty weather. Best part of the day is coming down the glen and thinking of a hot bath ahead and a Scotch and a good dinner. The thought of eighty degrees of frost in the North-west Territories makes my blood run cold. D'you know' – he turned to Miss Pink – 'they didn't have down clothing when Robert was young?'

'You'd have coped superbly,' Esme assured him. 'Robert did. No one knows what they're capable of until they're stretched.'

'You mean few people realise their potential?' Flora asked. 'We're all inadequate personalities?'

Miss Pink studied the child carefully. The tone had been innocent, but not the sense. Flora was either old for her years or considerably older than she looked.

Esme had hesitated. She answered carefully. 'Few people do realise their potential, but I don't think that makes them inadequate.'

'Why not?' Flora asked.

'Let's say they don't try hard enough.' Esme's tone became schoolmarmish. 'Our potential should always be beyond our reach—'

'What's yours?' Flora interrupted.

Esme checked and gave a small gasping laugh. 'It's not

always revealed to us. I said no one knows what they're capable of until they direct their powers.'

'You mean like you radiate power, a kind of laser, and hope to pick up a target?'

'You lost me.' Ranald was shaking his head. 'What's there to get so intense about?'

'It's not an *aggressive* concept.' Flora's eyes widened. 'Or is it?' she asked of Esme who shook her head, momentarily silenced.

Coline excused herself and left the room. Flora said sweetly, 'Would you like to live in Sgoradale, Miss Pink?'

'No.' It was too curt. She elucidated. 'There's a combination of violence and decadence that grates on me. I would find it an uncomfortable place to spend any length of time.'

'Violence?' Ranald repeated. 'Decadence?'

Flora and Esme were staring – the one delighted, the other angry. Miss Pink realised that she was on her third sherry, and that on an empty stomach. Nevertheless, she was committed.

'The violence is in the elements,' she explained, 'and a form of decadence in the sense that here is a remote community leading a leisurely life without stress. I wouldn't feel stretched here. That's one person's opinion, but you did ask.'

'You'd be bored,' Flora said flatly.

'Our lives aren't leisurely,' Esme protested. 'There's too much to do. I'm run off my feet. Not that I don't love every minute of it,' she added quickly.

'I'm a man of leisure,' Ranald admitted, 'but only because I'm well looked after. I'm a lazy fellow, but I'm never bored. Always something to do, y'know: fishing, shooting and so on. Never idle.'

'Decadent,' Flora mused. 'I like it. We sound like Roman emperors – beautiful and wicked, and into unspeakable perversions.'

'Now what?' Coline asked from the doorway. 'I make one entrance to a suggestion of glue sniffing, now this. Miss Pink has raised the tone of our *soirées*. Shall we continue this discussion at the table?'

They rose and trooped out of the drawing room, their silent

passage creating the effect of a subdued procession, or at the least, thoughtful.

'Seriously,' Flora began when they were seated – all but Esme, who had disappeared. 'Seriously, doesn't decadence go with violence?'

'It bothers me,' Miss Pink said happily, her appraisal of the silver, the napkins and the range of glasses having suggested that she was about to be served something better than 'meat and two veg.' even though the cook was on holiday. She gave them an embarrassed smile. 'You lead such cosy lives in contrast with the elemental forces around you. I couldn't accept that situation. I'm more at home in a place like the American West, where people fit their environment: wild men in a wild land. Most of them own guns because no system of law can be imposed on a wilderness. I believe those Westerners who tell me that many more crimes occur, even serious ones, than come to light.'

'That's true of any country,' Coline said.

Esme entered with a tray and went round the table serving plates of smoked salmon.

'Home-caught,' Ranald beamed. 'And Campbell smoked it.'

But Flora was like a young dog after sticks. She caught the one her mother had thrown. 'There are unreported crimes in Sgoradale?' She was incredulous. 'You just said nothing ever happened here except weather.'

'Not Sgoradale, but generally speaking. No doubt in Glasgow. . . . Do you know how many people go missing every year?'

Flora leaned her elbows on the table. 'No. How many?'

'I don't know, but thousands.'

'You think they're all murdered?'

'A significant proportion of them.'

'So where are their bodies?'

Ranald lumbered round the table filling their glasses. Coline looked at Miss Pink. 'Your cue, I think,' she murmured.

'You could become a mystery writer,' she told Flora, 'or a forensic pathologist. You have an enquiring mind. May one ask your age?'

21

'I'm sixteen.' The girl regarded her levelly. 'What happens to the bodies?'

Miss Pink wasted no time on surprise; she was now in her element. 'Murder is easy,' she said. 'It's disposal of the body that's the difficult part.' She took a sip of her wine and glanced at her host, who was watching anxiously. 'A Traminer?' she ventured. 'A nice choice.' She turned back to Flora. There were candles on the table, augmenting the low side lights. The girl still looked twelve years old. 'Well,' she resumed, 'bodies have been put through stone crushers and become part of a motorway; they've been baled inside cars and reduced to cubes of scrap metal in a breaker's yard. You know about corpses in cement foundations, of course, and animal feeding stuffs. Do you want more?'

Flora smiled. 'That'll do for starters.'

The conversation veered. 'Why do you need a policeman here?' Miss Pink asked generally. 'Surely there aren't enough inhabitants to justify a constable?'

'It's a bigger community than you think,' Ranald told her. 'There are large families crammed into small houses. At one time the young people left to find work, but now they stay. Those already in the towns get priority for any jobs and, goodness knows, there's a high rate of unemployment in the towns.'

'There were some motor bikes about on Saturday night. They were local youths?'

He nodded. 'There are the crofts on the lighthouse road, and a number around that you don't see, hidden in pockets away from the Lamentation Road. But there's no crime, as such; however, that could well be because of a police presence. And there's the harbour; boats put in for shelter or to unload a catch. In summer the population can quadruple, what with yachtsmen and caravans and visitors in the holiday cottages. Knox keeps a high profile in the season, particularly where ladies are concerned. The rest of the time I'd be hard put to say what he does, or where he is.' People smiled at that. Miss Pink's silence was polite but curious.

It was Coline who enlightened her. 'One morning the police

22

car was parked in the nurse's drive. That was all. I mean very early, at dawn. And it stayed there until Knox collected it, apparently when he got up and realised it wasn't outside his house.'

Miss Pink preserved a careful silence.

'The implication being that he'd spent the night in the nurse's house,' Ranald said. 'Of course, he hadn't. Who'd go home and leave his car behind, particularly a police car?'

'A practical joke?' Miss Pink asked.

'Rather a naughty one.' Coline stared into her wine. 'Knox is a lady's man, and Anne Wallace . . . In a place like this, one has to be quite extraordinarily discreet, and Knox is. I think everyone is, including Nurse Wallace. Putting the police car in her drive was . . . offensive; it was the action of someone not just calling attention to an extra-marital affair, but also to the cover-up.'

A silence followed, until Ranald said tactlessly, 'We have some amusing moments in Sgoradale. Remember the streaker?'

Coline said, 'Like the police car, that was a nine-second wonder, dear. If you're on the loch in summer, you can see naked people sunbathing all over the place.'

'He was in the *car park*!' Ranald turned to Miss Pink. 'Feller came galloping back to his car, starkers, couldn't get in – no keys, d'you see – ran up to a couple, goodness knows what he said, they didn't wait: chap started up and drove off like greased lightning. So the naked man disappears, comes back in a few minutes wearing a bin-liner!'

'What had happened?' Miss Pink asked, more curious than amused.

'Dunno. Lost his clothes. Those Hell's Angels were around – no doubt they stole 'em for a lark.'

'Who was the witness?' she asked. Ranald stared. 'Who told you the story? Someone had to be watching.'

'Another motorist was sitting in his car changing a film. He was in the pub that evening; next day the whole village knew.'

'So if he lost his clothes and his car keys, he lost his wallet too?'

'Evidently.' Ranald sobered and stared at her in the silence.

23

'And he didn't report it to Knox,' he said in wonder. 'Why was that?'

'Are you sure he didn't report it?'

'No,' Flora said, 'he didn't. Hamish would have told me. He's Knox's son,' she informed Miss Pink. 'He helps with the ponies. The man got into his car eventually by breaking a window. There was a lot of that laminated glass in the car park; I was down there next day picking up litter.'

'You didn't tell us,' Ranald said.

'It wasn't important.'

After the smoked salmon there was a saddle of venison and with it they drank a powerful burgundy. An association of ideas prompted Miss Pink to ask if the district nurse had enough work to keep her occupied.

'More than Knox has,' Coline said. 'There's a lot of elderly people and she travels a long way south, and inland. In summer time, like everyone else, she can be overworked: anything from sunburn to adder bites. The nearest doctor is fifteen miles away, at Morvern. Have you met the nurse?'

'Not yet. I've seen her in the distance. Not young, I would say.'

'Middle-aged but sprightly. Quite a good nurse on the whole, wouldn't you say, darling?'

Ranald shrugged. 'She took some stitches out of my foot; that's all the professional contact I've had. Haven't heard any complaints. Pleasant enough woman socially; knows her place. What's this?' – as Esme brought a bowl to the table – 'Blaeberry fool. You'll like that, Miss Pink. Cream from our own Jersey.'

The evening ended with Esme Dunlop insisting on walking Miss Pink home, an offer that could not be refused because they both went the same way. As they descended the drive by the light of torches, Esme took the older woman's arm and squeezed it companionably. 'It's a bit rough,' she said. 'Can't have you going down, can we?'

Miss Pink stopped and detached herself. 'I prefer to make my own way.'

'I didn't mean to annoy you.' They moved on slowly. 'Do I

intimidate you?' Esme pressed with anxious curiosity.

Miss Pink considered the question. 'A little,' she admitted. 'I think you dislike being alone and you avoid the condition by cleaving to people who are stronger than yourself. It's rather overpowering.'

'Rubbish. I'm a big hefty lady who crashes in where angels fear to tread and I scared the daylights out of you. Come on, own up. There are a lot of eccentric characters round here and you'll have to learn to live with us.' On the rough drive they wavered towards each other, touched and sheered away. 'You come from an undemonstrative family, right?' Esme's tone was roguish.

'And you?' Miss Pink asked.

'Me? What?'

'What is your background?'

'My mother's dead. My father's alive – in a nursing home. He's senile; I can't stand him.'

'How does he feel towards you?'

'It's mutual.' Esme hated the tables being turned. Before she could regain that equilibrium which could be so infuriating, Miss Pink pressed her advantage: 'And what brought you to Sgoradale?'

'Coline put an advertisement in *The Lady*. That was eight years ago.'

'You do more than secretarial work, I'm told.'

'I virtually run the place.' She seemed to take it for granted that she should be discussed by her employers. 'I'm one of the family now; in fact, they *are* my family. I don't know what they'd do without me.'

'You've made yourself indispensable.'

'Do I detect a note of criticism?'

'I was stating a fact. Isn't it correct?'

'Well, yes, but it's traditional for these old families to have a steward to run the house and estate, even—' she laughed deprecatingly '—even their lives to some extent.'

'Sir Ranald's is an old family?'

'No. The baronetcy was created only in 1902. His grandfather was a jute merchant and made a pile of money, but now there's nothing left except the title. And Ranald, of course.'

'How did Lady MacKay lose her first husband?'

'He ran off with a television actress, which is why Coline has custody of Flora. Not that Flora wouldn't prefer to be with her father in London, but I don't expect an actress in her twenties wants a sixteen-year-old step-daughter under her feet.'

'Why isn't Flora at school?'

'She left, and refuses to go back. Her mother's got a problem with that child. It's virtually a one-parent family, as you saw. Flora has no respect for her step-father, and there's not enough to amuse her in Sgoradale. She neglects her ponies, borrows her mother's car – or Ranald's, or the Land Rover – and disappears for days at a time.'

'How does she . . . square the police?'

Esme gave a snort of derision. 'She runs circles round Knox, the same as she does with her mother and step-father.'

'And yourself?' Miss Pink asked innocently.

'An armed truce. I'll stand no nonsense from Miss MacKenzie, and she knows it. I won't have those ponies neglected, but I can't force her to look after them, so I do it myself – like everything else that's important.' She changed the subject. 'I see Anne Wallace is either dog-tired or has run out of library books. Her light's out and usually she reads until midnight.'

They stopped and looked along the street which shimmered softly in the starlight. The night was calm. From the open sea came a whisper of water round the skerries.

'You'd love it here,' Esme said. 'You should give lectures. I'll draft a notice and have it printed in Inverness. We'll put on shows in Morvern and Ullapool; the whole district will turn out—'

'I don't lecture.'

'Oh, but you must! You have an excellent speaking voice, a good command of English and a vivid imagination—'

But Miss Pink had gone.

Chapter 3

'And forty Embassy, please.'

'You smoke too much, Debbie.' Rose Millar reached for the cigarettes and started totting up the bill. Miss Pink, awaiting her turn in the store, studied Debbie Campbell: a thin pale woman in jeans and an Icelandic sweater. She turned, murmured some response to Miss Pink's greeting, hesitated, then left the store.

Miss Pink bought a loaf and milk, exchanged views on the virtues of wholemeal bread and the likelihood of the weather breaking, then stepped outside to find Debbie standing a discreet distance from her open door. The woman said quickly, 'I work at the big house: Debbie Campbell. You talked to my husband yesterday.' Her eyes flickered to the doorway.

'I did,' Miss Pink said. 'Won't you come in?'

'I shan't take up your time; it's just that if you want to go out with Campbell, I'll tell him. I'm on my way home now.'

'Is there much to see on the loch?' Miss Pink knew that there was not at this time of year, but then that wasn't why the woman wanted to speak to her. 'I'm afraid I'd be taking your husband away from his work.'

'He does pretty much as he pleases.'

'A good workman is worth his weight in gold in a remote place.'

'He's a good worker, I'll say that for him. Mind if I smoke?'

Poker-faced, Miss Pink said she didn't and found the ash-tray she'd put in the sideboard. 'How long have you lived here?' she asked as they sat either side of the empty grate.

'Ten years. We've got two kids, a boy and a girl. They go to school in Morvern; you'll have seen the bus.' It went along the lighthouse road, turned and came back, picking up children from the crofts. The kids were happy at school, Debbie said, happy in Sgoradale: 'They're too young to know better – ten and nine.'

27

Miss Pink was suddenly effusive. 'And both you and your husband have good jobs! There's no bother about unemployment if people are prepared to work. And to travel. You had no worries about settling here in the first place?'

'I didn't have much choice. There was a baby on the way and Lady MacKay, she offered me a job in the house, and in a while Campbell was finding enough work to keep him busy.'

'You fell on your feet – but you must have had to work hard to stay there.'

Debbie sighed and stared out of the doorway. A marmalade cat had come to sit on the step and wash his face; the only movement was a long red paw pressing and releasing a velvet ear.

'So what's the problem?' Miss Pink asked.

Debbie's shoulders drooped. Her gaze returned from the foreshore to the questioner. 'You talked to him,' she said accusingly; Miss Pink nodded. Debbie's eyes wavered. 'I don't have no one to talk to.'

'What's wrong with Lady MacKay?'

'She couldn't care less.'

Miss Pink's eyebrows rose a fraction. 'There's Miss Swan.'

'She likes Campbell – but she don't have to live with him.'

'You mean he's not likeable?'

'No! I mean she's not bothered.'

'Like Lady MacKay?'

'Oh, no! They're opposites. Lady MacKay doesn't *care* if people are worried or even a bit scared. She's got her own life to lead and can't be bothered with working folk. They're the lairds, aren't they? But Miss Swan doesn't take no notice of – all this talk about . . . ' Debbie bit her lip. There was a sibilant mutter.

'Russians?' Miss Pink asked.

Debbie gave her a hard look. 'Is there anything in it?'

'In your husband's . . . speculations? There's been a great fuss in London about fishermen coming ashore in Ullapool with no one keeping a check on how many return to their ships.'

Debbie nodded. 'They said so on TV. But there's no call for Campbell to suspect everyone is a Russian spy!'

Miss Pink smiled; she'd already guessed that she filled that role herself. 'If you assume that some fishermen are spies, it's reasonable to think they could make contact with spies already in position – sleepers.'

'He's been interested in spies all his life. It's a long time to have a hobby like that, isn't it?'

'Some men play with model trains all their lives.'

'You mean *toy* trains? When they're grown-up?'

'They convert their lofts and spend hours running trains round tracks.'

'But aren't they a bit – weird?'

'On the contrary; some hold down highly responsible jobs – professional men.'

Debbie tried to relate this to her own problem and failed. 'It's not the same. He's started making things up. I've known him since he was in his first job; he knows I know he's telling lies but it doesn't seem to matter.'

'How do the children take it?'

'Like a game.'

'It is a game, like the trains. Does he talk much about his interests outside the family?'

'Didn't he talk to you?'

'He referred to contracts.'

'Oh, my God! Could *you* cope with it? I mean – getting the fidgets when he's watching TV, saying, "I'll take a turn outside. I didn't hear anything; I just want to make *sure*. . . ." Knowing he's lying there listening in bed when an owl calls. . . . He'll get up and look out of the window, standing well back, then he'll go in the kids' room and I know he's looking out of that window. It's *not* a game. I'm scared, miss.'

She sent Debbie away with the suggestion that she should discuss his behaviour with her husband. To her amazement that seemed to satisfy the woman. A trouble shared, Miss Pink thought, strolling across the road to sit on an upturned dinghy and contemplate the birds. After a while she became aware of the boat, *Blue Zulu*, drawn up below her – and here was Campbell himself, the old van emerging from the bend. It stopped and he came towards her, a figure of menace.

'You been talking to my wife,' he said, not bothering to lower his voice.

'Good morning, Mr Campbell.' Her tone was a rebuke, but he was far too angry to heed it.

'What was she telling you?'

A youth on a bicycle swept out of the policeman's drive and started along the street. He slowed suddenly and swerved across the road.

'You talked about me?' Campbell was grinning unpleasantly.

'Debbie's frightened,' Miss Pink said.

'Of me?' He was astonished.

'Of course not.' Observing the boy, who was now leaning over the side of a beached dinghy doing something under a thwart, Miss Pink took the plunge. 'But if you've got yourself involved in something you can't handle, there are the children to be considered. She's worried about the effect on them. They may think of it as a game. She knows better. The sensation of being watched can be terrifying.'

'Who's watching her?'

'Not her. You. Who's outside your cottage at night?'

He considered this carefully, all signs of anger gone. Miss Pink was sympathetic, but she thought of the children and stuck to her guns. 'I'm puzzled,' she said. 'I take it that you haven't done anything illegal?'

He glanced at her sharply. He'd be unaccustomed to being taken seriously by someone of her stamp.

'Because if you've done nothing illegal,' she went on, 'one assumes that the other people have – the watchers. Why are they after you?'

His face cleared. 'It's a long story,' he began, 'and complicated. It's like this—' He bit his thumb and stared out to sea. He looked around, his gaze lingering on the lad by the boat, then passing on. No one was abroad in the street. 'I was approached by the police,' he resumed. 'Recruited for undercover work. You don't believe that, do you?'

'Go on.' Her eyes were attentive.

'They approached me in Glasgow. I used to drink in a bar by the university. The Special Branch needed someone to infiltrate the subversives: anarchists, communists, ethnics, like that. I was perfect for the job; everyone thought I was a student. So I became an agent.' He regarded her without expression.

'So who is watching your cottage?'

But he'd decided to retract. 'I don't think anyone is at this moment. It could have been my imagination. We're trained to be on the alert all the time. It's all stress; you get so you see things that aren't there.'

'Who did you think it was?'

'Someone from the Glasgow days, someone I'd put away, and he'd been released and come looking for me.'

'The police wouldn't help?'

He looked meaningly at the lad who was still tinkering with the boat. 'That's the police,' he said in scorn, 'sending his son out to keep tabs on me. Special Branch has got no time for the uniforms, and Gordon Knox can't keep the local lads in order, let alone deal with a professional hit man. No, you settle your own scores in Sgoradale.'

'You said it was your imagination.'

'I said it *could* be – this time.'

She suppressed a sigh. 'It could be more . . . comfortable to share your anxiety—'

'Who says I'm anxious? I'm just on my guard.'

'If you talk it over with your wife, there are two pairs of eyes—'

'There are three pairs already. The kids know what to watch out for.'

'Mr Campbell! If the children are in your confidence, then your wife should be. She's worried sick.'

'OK,' he said, casual as a child. 'I'll go and have it out with her.'

He turned and loped to his van. Amazed at his tone and not at all pleased with his turn of phrase, she stared after him as he drove away, then she looked towards the Knox lad. He had mounted his bicycle and was riding slowly in the direction that Campbell had taken.

She went home to her domestic chores. While she was washing up she glanced out of the kitchen window to see what

31

appeared to be a string of beads moving diagonally across the escarpment. As she watched, the leader turned at an acute angle and the rest followed in its tracks. They were sheep and they must be on a path that was invisible from below. That would repay investigation.

After lunch, she followed the river upstream and climbed past a series of waterfalls to emerge on the open moor. She crossed the river by dry boulders and trudged through the heather to the lip of the escarpment. Following its edge, she came to the track where she'd seen the sheep and looked straight down on the roofs of the lodge. Beyond it were the grounds, less wooded than they appeared to be from sea level, more like parkland. Two riders were threading their way through spires of American spruce.

They halted. They must be talking for the horses swung about, anxious to be away, but the people were deep in conversation and ignored the fretting of their mounts. Another person was coming up the lodge drive, accompanied by a diminutive orange speck: Alec and Baby on their afternoon constitutional.

The sun was warm and she watched idly. She saw Alec approach the house but, before the drive widened to the forecourt, he took off across the lawns in the direction of the river. Where the lawns ended and the parkland began, man and dog disappeared behind trees, to emerge again – Alec plodding like an old man.

The riders were between Alec and the river. Now they were in motion again, riding away from him a half-mile or so ahead, and each party hidden from the other. The riders were still restraining their horses and even at this distance a horseman could sense the animals' frustration as they walked with short stiff steps. A head was tossed, haunches swung out. It happened once too often, too near a tree; there was a flurry of bucking and the riders faced each other, the ponies backing and filling. Suddenly one broke away – amazingly fast it seemed to the watcher on the scarp; she saw an arm rise and fall as the rider whipped his mount to full gallop: down the path up which Alec Millar was coming.

Miss Pink watched in horror. He must hear the hoofbeats, she thought; he's got time to jump clear. Alec had stopped. The horse exploded from a group of firs, closing the gap, but before they collided – fast horse and stationary man – Alec must have moved. There was a space between them as the horse passed, but the speed checked dramatically. There was a scream. The shape of the horse had changed; it had gone down.

Miss Pink raised the binoculars. The horse was climbing to its feet, the saddle hanging below its belly. The policeman's son was standing, clutching his arm and staring at big, childlike Alec who was advancing on him like a gorilla, with what appeared to be a club in one hand. Of the poodle there was no sign.

Everything was in slow motion and Miss Pink had time to reflect that she could be the only witness when suddenly the scene changed. Young Knox was running through the trees and Alec, starting after him, lurched back, took a wild swipe at the horse which plunged away and took off at a gallop, the saddle bumping between its legs.

Miss Pink released her breath and lowered the binoculars. She looked to her right and saw a tiny figure moving rhythmically round a green space: Flora MacKenzie taking her pony over jumps. If that had been a lovers' spat, she thought, it had been one-sided. This one wasn't bothered.

She descended the green track and worked her way through the parkland until she reached the path she was looking for. This was used regularly by ponies, but their tracks were overlaid by the gouged imprints of an animal at full gallop. She turned north towards the river and, after some casting about, discovered the place where the incident had occurred. There was the indentation made by the pony when it fell and rolled, and there was the broken branch which must be the club that Alec had brandished, but there was nothing else and for that she was thankful.

As she approached her cottage, a woman came bustling down the nurse's drive and hurried ahead to turn in at the Post Office. Miss Pink unlocked her front door and left it ajar. It was five-thirty. Mindful that Beatrice Swan had invited her to dine at six-thirty, she went upstairs to run her bath.

She was changed and downstairs again when the nurse passed the open door. Miss Pink called to her. She turned back: a slim neat person, her hair all but concealed by the uniform cap, her face unremarkable except for the eyes: hooded, large and grey, enhanced by careful make-up. Miss Pink introduced herself and Anne Wallace responded pleasantly and with no sign of impatience.

'I was on the cliff,' Miss Pink said, with a gesture as incomplete as the statement. 'Did Alec have an accident?'

'Not exactly.' The accent suggested the nurse came from the Hebrides. 'His dog was killed. He's – very unhappy about it. Did you see what happened?'

'Probably less than Alec did. I was over half a mile away and they were in the trees. What does Alec say?'

'He's in no condition to tell us.'

'A convulsion?'

The nurse stalled. 'He's unwell. He came home with the dog in his arms, and crying, so you see . . . '

'I know his history from Mrs Millar. Is there anything I can do?'

'No, Rose can cope. She phoned me because he was worse than usual, with the dog and all. I mean—'

'She was afraid that the convulsion would be worse,' Miss Pink interpreted. 'Shocking for anyone, of course, but worse for Alec.'

'Who did it?'

'Oh, no one. Not a *person*. The dog must have been in the way of a pony.'

'Who was riding it, or do you mean the pony was loose?' Miss Pink did not respond. 'Alec will tell us when he's better,' the nurse said. 'It was either Flora MacKenzie or Hamish Knox.'

'It was the boy.'

'He did it deliberately?'

'No. The pony went down and the boy must have taken quite a nasty tumble, with the speed he was going.'

'And then what happened?'

'Why, Alec went for him and young Knox ran away. I thought, from a distance you know, that no harm had been

34

done, except a few bruises to horse and rider. I did hear a scream, however.'

'That was the dog. It was all Alec could say when he reached home: "She screamed." He's not going to forget it in a hurry.'

'That was an understatement,' Beatrice said. 'Alec's world revolved around that animal. He told me once, and without a trace of self-consciousness, that he thought of her as his "kid sister". His words.'

They were in the sitting room at Feartag. This evening Beatrice was in fine pink wool and in the lamplight her skin looked like parchment, the deep eye sockets stressing her age and fragility.

'Another dog would hardly fill the gap,' Miss Pink mused.

'He'd kill it.' The statement was without emotion and Miss Pink was amazed. On reflection she agreed that this would be likely.

'You know how his mind works,' she conceded. 'I didn't tell Anne Wallace this, but he would have attacked young Knox – he'd picked up a heavy branch – but the boy ran away. So then he aimed a blow at the pony.'

'A natural reaction for anyone, and Alec has less control than most people.'

'What can his relationship with young Knox be now?'

'Someone may have to accompany him on his walks for a while, but if there's no dog he won't take walks. The answer might be to send him away for a time, on a supervised holiday.'

'Or Hamish might be sent away for a while?'

'Hamish will do as he pleases.'

'His parents have little influence?'

Beatrice regarded her guest speculatively. 'Have you heard about the police car being found in Anne Wallace's drive at dawn? The village people pretend it was Hell's Angels, who were also supposed to be breaking into cars around that time. But they wouldn't have known about Knox and the nurse, and they didn't have access to the keys of the police car. But if local youths moved that car, then the keys still had to be handed to them, and replaced.'

'Why would Hamish want to do a thing like that?'

'As a practical joke. The village has known – I should say some of us have known – for a long time that Knox was more friendly with Anne Wallace than he should be. I suspect his own wife knew. But Joan Knox is a doormat and even if she weren't, she might hope that the affair would run its course. Be that as it may, people knew, but with the discretion that you get in small communities nothing was said, at least in public. There was no gossip. We have to live together. Turning a blind eye is a survival tactic in a place like Sgoradale. Hamish doesn't have that tactic.'

'Have there been other incidents?'

After a while Beatrice said, 'There are telephone calls.'

'What kind?'

'The type where you pick up the phone and no one speaks. Sometimes there is a laugh. The phone at the other end is put down with a clatter.'

'A pay phone or private?'

'A private line.'

'And the laugh?'

'Muffled, breathless, more of a snigger.'

'Does anyone else get such calls?'

'I haven't asked. It's not the kind of thing one talks to people about.'

'How long has this been going on?'

'For a few weeks. I've had two of them – that is, two that I've answered. They come late at night. The first two times I came downstairs; now I let the phone ring and I lie there, listening. It rings for ages. One gets more and more disturbed. I find the whole business absolutely monstrous!' She shuddered and bit her lip.

Miss Pink said calmly, 'And you think Hamish is making these calls?'

'Oh, no. No!' Beatrice was shocked. 'It's one thing to play a bad joke on your father, but quite another to set out to terrify a woman living alone. But someone's making them, certainly. I'm inclined to think it's some children on the lighthouse road – older children, adolescents.'

'You've not talked to Coline about it?'

'No. I find Coline superficial and peculiarly arrogant. She's sociable, but she's more concerned with her books than with real people. Of course the books are money-spinners and sometimes I wonder if Coline's only interested in money. She seems to have little feeling, even for her family. No, I don't confide in Coline. And as for Ranald, he would be gallant and get on the telephone to the Chief Constable – and what could he do? This would never have happened when Robert was alive.'

'Why not? Even he couldn't have done anything about an anonymous caller.'

'You don't understand. The call isn't dangerous; it's a signal – that someone is out there who knows you're alone, who could even have seen the lights go on in your house as you went downstairs to answer the phone. *You're being watched.* He's revelling in your fear; fear that he's going to break in and . . . you know the rest. None of it could have happened with a man in the house, a man whom everyone knew was a splendid shot and without fear.'

Miss Pink had stiffened at mention of someone watching the house, but all she said was, 'Are his guns still here?'

'Yes. Locked up of course. But a gun's pointless unless you're prepared to use it.'

'It might be a good idea to put in some shooting practice. Do you have a firearms certificate?'

'Yes. One has to keep down the rabbits and grey squirrels.'

A timer rang in the kitchen and brought an end to the conversation. Over dinner, Miss Pink gave an account of her meetings with the Campbells earlier that day. At the end she asked, 'What do you feel about these stories of Campbell's involvement with the Special Branch, and sinister people lurking in the wings?'

Beatrice shrugged. 'I ignore it. To be frank, I find it annoying because I'm the one who is actually getting telephone calls, while with Campbell the persecution is all in his mind. Then I've caught myself wondering whether I could have dreamed those calls, whether I could be going senile. So I discourage Campbell's fantasies; they come too close to home.'

After dinner they had the slide show. Polar wastes were not Miss Pink's favourite kind of country but they were magnificent to look at, particularly from the comfort of an armchair, and Beatrice took obvious delight in the pictures.

'When I see that glacier on the Greenland ice-cap, I hear his voice talking about "crevasses like green glass". I repeat it deliberately; it brings him back, if he ever went away.'

As she was preparing to take her leave, Miss Pink considered whether this was the right moment to suggest that Beatrice should send for an expert to advise her on security. She caught the other woman's eye.

'Don't worry,' Beatrice said. 'When you look at it sensibly I've nothing to lose. I don't even have an animal as a hostage to fortune.'

Chapter 4

'And how is Alec?'

On the other side of the counter Rose Millar stiffened. 'As well as can be expected. Nurse told us what you said happened. Are you certain it wasn't done deliberate?'

'There's no question,' Miss Pink assured her. 'The pony was going full pelt; Hamish was lucky not to be seriously injured.'

'He should have controlled the beast.'

Rose was a small round woman and when she was angry she looked like a fiery robin. Suddenly the fire left her. 'It's their land,' she said miserably. 'I s'pose the lad can do what he likes when he's exercising their horses. Alec was in the wrong being there, but Lady Coline never minded no one walking through the park.'

'No one's to blame,' Miss Pink said. 'It was an accident.'

'*He's* not going to believe that.' Rose jerked her head at the ceiling. 'He's lying there, in bed. He won't eat, he won't talk. He don't cry any more though.'

Duncan Millar appeared in the doorway that led to the living quarters: a thickset man in his sixties with a beard, wisps of grey hair showing below his old deerstalker. Like most local men he was a jack of all trades – ghillie, fisherman, estate worker. Now he was out of his depth. 'He says he'll kill him,' he told his wife.

'He's talking then?' Rose was relieved. 'You mind the shop, and I'll take him his breakfast. I knew he'd come round; it was the shock.'

'We can't let him out.' Duncan was morose.

Rose's eyes went from him to Miss Pink as the meaning penetrated. 'One of us will have to go with him. But he'll be wanting to stay in for a time, get his strength back. His turns take a lot out of him.'

The post van drew up outside and the driver entered with the mail. In the ensuing bustle Miss Pink stepped back and collided with Esme Dunlop, who had come in from the street. They apologised to each other, Esme continuing with voluble explanations of her presence involving a parcel of bulbs and then – 'How is Alec?' she asked abruptly.

Miss Pink told her what she knew – leaving out the part about Alec's brandishing the tree branch – while Rose busied herself with the mail. Duncan had retreated to the back premises.

'You saw it all,' Esme said, her eyes gleaming.

'From the top of the cliff. How did you know that?'

'I was visiting Anne Wallace last evening.' She smiled indulgently. 'Quite simple, you see. No spying involved. Is that parcel for me, Rose?'

'No, Miss Dunlop, but I did see a letter here somewhere.'

'I'll hang on; I need some bicarb. I eat too fast, that's my problem—'

'Here you are, Miss Dunlop.'

'I don't know this writing,' Esme said, taking a small white envelope from her. 'It's probably some poor old soul who wants me to sort out her electricity bill or something.' She smiled ruefully. 'What it is to be a secretary!' She unfolded a sheet of paper absently, but as she read her lips parted and she lost colour. Miss Pink could see that the paper bore a short message in letters of differing size and type. Her eyes met Esme's appalled stare and then the woman turned and blundered out of the shop.

Rose was occupied with the postman and showed no interest in the scene. Miss Pink stepped outside and saw Esme running towards the cottages on the bend of the Lamentation Road. She reached her front door, pushed it open and stumbled over the sill. The door slammed.

Miss Pink telephoned Beatrice Swan, thanked her for her hospitality of last evening and returned the invitation. She conveyed the latest news of Alec and said that she had to go to Inverness: 'My typewriter's jammed. Can I bring you anything?'

'Please. I need vanilla pods, plain chocolate, leaf gelatine. I'll tell you where to go . . . '

By ten o'clock she was on the Lamentation Road, coming over the moors on yet another glorious morning. She found herself wondering what she might do when the weather broke. Was it to be the Mediterranean or back to Arizona? She couldn't return to her house in Cornwall because that was let – much to the chagrin of her housekeeper, who was looking after the tenants as well as the property.

She realised with astonishment that she had given no thought to the outside world for days on end. She had been absorbed by Sgoradale and its inhabitants. Now the outer world impinged and she felt as if she'd been away for months, not days.

The road dipped and sank over the long brown swells. A mile or so ahead there was something on the tarmac, and as the gap closed it was revealed as a hitch-hiker. At first she thought she was overtaking a tramp, his belongings in a bedding roll on a string, then she saw that he was carrying one of the large strap bags now favoured by trendy travellers. He turned and thumbed the car; it was no man, but Flora MacKenzie.

She was wearing the baggy pants, the chic sweater that she had worn at the dinner party, but a navy watch cap was pulled low on her forehead. Miss Pink stopped and the girl opened the passenger door.

'Good morning! Lovely to see you. Can you give me a lift?'

'How far are you going?'

'Edinburgh?'

'I can take you to Inverness.'

'Right. I can catch a train from there.'

'You don't drive?' Miss Pink said as they started off again.

Flora stared at her. 'I'm only sixteen.'

'Of course. Why didn't someone run you to Inverness?'

'My mother, you mean? Why should she? I wouldn't expect it.'

'She does know you're going to Edinburgh?'

Flora giggled. 'Do I look like a runaway? Mum knows. I'm staying with a friend – very respectable people; her father's a barrister.'

'But hitching! Don't you have the bus fare?'

'Hitching's more fun; you never know who you're going to meet.'

'That's the point.'

'You mean rape. Miss Pink, you've *seen* Sgoradale. D'you really think it's swarming with rapists?'

'You only need one, and everyone has to start somewhere, even rapists. And rape can lead to murder.' Flora looked bored. So Miss Pink changed the subject. 'So what's the next step? University?'

'You need A-levels for that. In any case, I see no point in my going up to university. What's it for?'

'Further education, perhaps. What's your interest?'

'If there's nothing else to do, you write, don't you?'

'Is that a deliberate insult, or thoughtlessness?'

'I'm so *sorry*!' She did look devastated. 'I meant the trash Mum churns out. You're a professional.' She stared anxiously at Miss Pink's profile.

'Forget about creative writing. Journalism might be the answer if you're interested in people—'

'Oh, I am!'

'So is there a plan in the short term, or am I probing?'

'I suppose I *am* one of the beautiful people – isn't that what you used to call us?' Flora smiled engagingly. 'I'm teasing you, but I'm used to being slapped down at home so I'm taking advantage. The fact is, I shan't be independent until I'm eighteen. Then I come into Grandmama MacKenzie's money – along with a castle in Angus. I'm an heiress.' Her lips twitched. 'So I'm hanging around, waiting. But I am considering training for something. It's just . . . there was no one to ask.'

'Training?'

Flora shot her a glance. 'How's this for a scenario? I train as a journalist, and when I'm eighteen I buy a newspaper?'

'What do your parents say?'

'My mother, you mean. She expects me to marry. The MacKenzies are old-fashioned and won't hear of me going into television or advertising, or catering for an up-market take-away. That would mean living away from home, and there are all kinds of evils lurking out there.'

'You'd have to leave home to study journalism.'

'It would have to be a residential college, or lodging with friends of Mum's. I'm a marketable property, a dynastic pawn. There, have I a way with words?'

'You have indeed.'

'So perhaps you would speak to my mother about a college?'

'And you do some homework in Edinburgh: go to libraries, read some careers books.'

'I could do that.'

Flora's interest was spiked with boredom. When animated it was as if she never talked to other adults. As they were crossing the bridge over the Beauly Firth, Miss Pink said, 'You're friendly with Hamish Knox.' Flora's face became set. 'I saw you riding with him yesterday,' she went on. 'Did he hurt himself when he came off?'

'He was shaken up a bit. Where were you?'

'I was on the cliff above your house. I had a bad moment; I anticipated the worst – that it would be Alec who was run down.'

Flora said nothing.

'Unfortunate about the dog,' Miss Pink added.

'Did it get kicked?'

'I suppose so. Or the pony fell on it.'

Flora was looking hard at her. 'Did it have to be put down?'

'No, it was killed instantly, or so I understand. Didn't you know?'

The girl stared through the windscreen. She sighed. 'I'm sorry. How would I know? Hamish came back to the yard, but he didn't know either. Alec attacked him and he ran away as fast as he could. And I've not spoken to Hamish since, so I didn't know about the dog. I'll bring a puppy back from Edinburgh and give it to Alec.'

'I shouldn't do that. Wait until he gets over his loss. And Hamish should be the one to make amends; he was whipping that pony like a madman.'

'He was? I didn't look back – we'd had words about the jumps. He wanted to raise them for the gelding – but you're not interested in shop talk. The point is, they're my ponies and I won't be dictated to, not by him anyway. I taught him to ride; no way is he going to tell me how to train my animals. He got mad.' Flora grinned. 'I guess I let the relationship get out of

43

hand. He got pushy yesterday and I had to come the *grande dame*.'

'And what does he plan to do with himself?' They were on the outskirts of Inverness and Miss Pink's attention was on the traffic.

'I've no idea. He's a drifter. No doubt he'll end up as an estate worker once he's learned to control his temper. Most of them do. End up working for us, I mean.'

Miss Pink dropped her passenger at the railway station and, Flora having declined an invitation to luncheon, lunched herself at the Station Hotel before setting out to find a man to mend her typewriter and to buy delicacies unobtainable on the West Coast. But the afternoon was warm and the city streets stank of exhaust fumes, so it was with relief that she crossed the last item from her list and, the boot stacked with boxes of food and drink, started back to Sgoradale.

She returned by a more westerly route than the central moors. The sun had set by the time she reached the coast and the tide was high. Water lay like pools of opal silk in coves where ragged stacks were silhouetted against the afterglow. As she came round the bend of the Lamentation Road, the lights of crofts were twinkling on the far side of the loch. When she pulled up on the turf and cut her engine, she could hear the water lapping a few yards away, and the air smelled of seaweed and salt.

After supper she relaxed in an armchair, a brandy at her elbow, *The Times* within reach. As she went to pick it up, she became aware of a sound in the kitchen, like someone knocking on the window pane.

Her thoughts flew to Esme Dunlop. There was no escape; her car was outside, her light was burning. She rose heavily and went to the kitchen. She was prepared for a face at the window pane so was not alarmed to see one, but there was no Cheshire cat grin and when she switched on the outer light and opened the back door, it was not Esme blinking in the glare but Ivar Campbell, and he looked terrified.

'The light,' he gasped. 'Put the light out.'

'Damn it,' protested Miss Pink. 'Pull yourself together. And don't give me orders.'

'Please! Let me in. Have you got a drink?'

'I'm on my way to bed.'

'I must have a drink.'

'The bar's open.'

He shook his head helplessly. Aware that she could be asking for trouble but too tired to argue, she retreated. 'Close the door,' she told him curtly. He did so, and bolted it.

She seated him beside the fire and gave him a tot of brandy. He was haggard: unshaven, dirty – black dirty. There were smears of soot on his face and hands. He didn't remove his cap. She waited but so did he, and the silence gave her time to select her course of action.

'Were you followed here?' she asked.

'There's no doubt of it.' The response was apathetic. She'd chosen correctly, not exciting him.

'And Debbie and the children? They're on their own?'

His eyes were desperate. 'You don't have to worry about them any more.'

A cold hand twisted her gut. She started to speak, but he was muttering about a fire. '*Fire?*' She heaved herself to her feet. 'Your house is on fire?'

'No!'

She checked and started to breathe deeply; she must not let him rile her. She sat down carefully.

'Are Debbie and the children safe?'

He wouldn't meet her eye. 'I guess so.'

'What does that mean?'

'It means I don't know! How would I know?' Now he did look at her: angry, bewildered, lost. 'She left me.'

'When?'

'Probably in the forenoon some time. I came home this afternoon and she was gone.'

'She'll come back.'

'She's taken all her clothes, and the kids' things. Someone took her away; she couldn't have carried all that stuff on her own.'

'You're not suggesting she's been abducted?'

He looked startled. 'I hadn't thought of that. You mean held to ransom?'

Miss Pink considered this reaction, then asked, 'What did you say about a fire?'

'The place was set fire to. It was in flames when I got home. I been fighting it, that's why I'm . . . like this.' He spread his filthy hands.

'It's still burning?'

'No, I managed to put it out.'

'Mr Campbell – Ivar – are you sure your wife and children are safe?' Someone should check which parts of this story were fact and which fantasy, she thought, although the soot on his face pointed to at least part of its being true. Nevertheless, soot can be transferred from a fire-back to the face.

'I didn't hear the fire brigade,' she said.

'By the time I could have got to a phone, the fire was out. I don't have a telephone.'

'No one helped you fight the fire?'

He was surprised. 'Don't you know where I live? In the woods beyond the car park. The place could have burned to the ground and no one the wiser except them that set the fire.'

'Why did they want to burn it?'

'Ah!' The exclamation conveyed deep satisfaction. 'They'd have hoped I was inside, but that wouldn't be all of it. They were after my records.'

'Records?'

'That's confidential.' He looked sly.

'Of course. So you haven't informed the police?'

'No way.'

'You've left the records unguarded at this moment?'

'The place is secure, and they won't try again tonight. They know I'll be waiting, and they'll be pretty sure I'm armed. Did you see any strange cars about today?'

'No. Wouldn't they want to read the records before they destroyed them?'

'That's a good point. Maybe they selected some, burned the others. The fire was started with paper; I was trained in forensics, so I could see how it started. They'd turned over the armchairs and put papers underneath and doused the lot with

46

petrol. The house stinks of it. I'll be printing the place, but I doubt they wore gloves.'

'You're taught to lift fingerprints too? But what use are they without comparison? Aren't these people strangers to you?'

'I'll tell you,' he said quietly. 'I got the feeling you could be the only one I can trust. I think there's a sleeper in this village. You know what a sleeper is?' She nodded. 'So I've collected all their prints over the years. They don't know, of course. But if it's a local tried to burn my place down, and me in it and all my records, I got my comparisons, see?'

Chapter 5

One of the obvious moves of the wife-killer is to tell his neighbours that the wife left of her own accord, taking all her clothes. The knowledge of this had been bothering Miss Pink since Campbell first told her that Debbie had left the village, and it continued to worry her throughout the night. She did get to bed eventually, after she sent Campbell home. Then she was inclined to doubt that the cottage had been on fire, because when she asked him where he intended to sleep he said that he would go home. He gave no indication that his house was uninhabitable.

He had left, using the front door quite openly, with no anxious glance to see what might be waiting for him outside. Watching him walk past the nurse's drive, illuminated by the last street light, his hands in his pockets, almost jaunty, she was struck by his change of mood. He appeared satisfied, as if he'd succeeded in his mission. To impress her, presumably, but in what respect? That he was a target for a killer, or cruelly treated by his wife?

She fell asleep quickly, only to wake an hour later convinced that Debbie had to be located. She went downstairs and sat over the dying fire with a cup of tea, considering whether she should go to the police or to Campbell's cottage. But if the man were merely riding his imagination on a loose rein, she didn't want some bumpkin of a policeman giving undue weight to her information. For all she knew, it could be the sympathetic hearing she gave his fantasies that was stimulating him to greater flights.

She didn't get to sleep again until the dawn showed behind her curtains, and then she slept late. She came downstairs feeling gritty and disgruntled and took her time over breakfast. She knew that she was resentful, not because her day was disrupted, but because she was indecisive.

The sputter of an outboard motor alerted her and she looked out of the open door to see *Blue Zulu* chugging down the loch. There could be little wrong if he were going fishing and, better still, she was free to investigate the cottage, to eliminate all doubt without danger or the fear of ridicule.

She drove up the Lamentation Road, passing the track which she now knew led to the car park, looking for another which would give access to the cottage, but there was none. She turned and came back to take the dusty trail to the car park. This was a space in the trees with a drive taking off from the far corner and a notice saying: PRIVATE PROPERTY. NO ACCESS. Within a hundred yards she came to a whitewashed cottage nestling under the escarpment, with a stone barn off to one side. There was no sign of fire.

She opened the gate and walked up a flagged path to the front door. She depressed the thumb latch, smiling as she re-membered Campbell's talk of fingerprints, but as she'd ex-pected, the door was locked.

She moved to the window on the left. There was a sink below it with dishes on a draining board, a mop, liquid soap. She could distinguish a plastic-topped table and four chairs. She glimpsed shelves, tins of food, crockery, pans, a cooker, a refrigerator.

She crossed to the window on the other side of the door, but there was no question of seeing inside this room. The glass had a smoky bloom that rendered it opaque. The little she could see of the inner sill was thick with soot.

A door slammed. She turned and saw a police car parked behind her Renault and a man in uniform approaching. He came up the path favouring her with a smile that lit his eyes. This was no country bumpkin. He was fair, with blue eyes and a small moustache. He was a fraction overweight, like a rugby player a little past his prime, but his uniform fitted him well. He held out his hand.

'Miss Pink, I believe. I'm Gordon Knox. You were looking for Campbell?'

'For his wife actually.' She returned the smile as she shook hands. She was greatly relieved; there were no more decisions to make – at least for the time being. Let Authority take over.

In the person of this man it seemed capable enough.

'Mrs Campbell went away yesterday,' he told her. He glanced at the smoky window. 'And that's not going to bring her back neither.'

'There's been a fire?' She drew it out.

'Did you meet Campbell yet?'

'Yes, we've had some conversation.'

'And I believe you've been a magistrate, ma'am?'

'I have.' She pitied anyone who tried to hide their past in a Highland village.

'So you'll have come across situations like this before?'

'I'm not sure that I know what the situation is, Mr Knox. There's been a fire, his wife has left . . . ' She trailed off and he met her eyes without subterfuge.

'Exactly. He set the fire.'

'How can you be certain?'

'You're not surprised, ma'am. And you don't need to be well acquainted with Mr Campbell to see he's an exhibitionist. He set the fire to bring his wife back.'

'I'd think it would only serve to drive her further away, particularly if she has the children with her.'

'She has the children. I called the school and she picked them up yesterday and didn't send them back this morning. She phoned the headmistress and told her she's taking them to her mother in Pitlochry.' He paused and regarded her with a mock seriousness which was suddenly illumined by his dazzling smile. 'You talked to Campbell. If he didn't tell you that he was involved with the Special Branch and that someone was gunning for him, it was only because he thought you were the Enemy.'

She nodded. 'So you think he started a fire to demonstrate to his wife that his fantasies were in fact reality? That's possible. A bitter quarrel could have been the cause of all this; it makes sense. Poor man. But how did you know? I didn't expect him to tell you about the fire.'

'He came to my house early this morning with a story about arsonists breaking in here yesterday afternoon.'

'There's no sign of a break-in.'

'He said they went to the back door. Shall we see?'

They walked round the cottage. A neat vegetable plot was laid out between the house and rough ground at the base of the cliff. A dustbin stood by the back door, the wood of which was raw and splintered beside the key-hole.

'He's thorough,' Knox said with grudging admiration. He depressed the thumb latch and the door gave slightly, then stopped solid. 'He's barred it with something, probably a piece of timber.'

Miss Pink removed the dustbin lid to reveal a garment which she lifted gingerly. It was a child's jersey, clean but ragged and unravelled. In the bottom of the black plastic liner were a number of tins, burned and flattened. Knox regarded her with amusement.

'She did turn up at the school,' he reminded her. 'In a taxi, and she telephoned the headmistress this morning. The man's unbalanced, but he's not a murderer.'

'Are you being indiscreet, Mr Knox?'

'This is the back of beyond, ma'am, and there aren't any witnesses to our conversation. We don't – in fact we can't – do things by the book in Sgoradale.'

'So why are you confiding in me?'

'I'm not telling you anything you don't know, just reassuring you a bit maybe. The reason Campbell came to me was because he wants this' – he gestured at the cottage – 'publicised. He doesn't know where his wife is; well, if he guesses she's gone to her mother's he's too intimidated by the family to follow her. What he wants is this incident to get in the papers and on television, so she'll know about it, be sorry she left, and come back.'

'That would be totally irrational,' Miss Pink murmured, 'and he's not. It's more like a cry for help: showing Debbie what she's forced him to do: retaliating, like a man threatening suicide because he's been rejected. What motive did he attribute to the arsonists?'

'First he tried to convince me that someone had meant for him to die in the fire, and when I said that wasn't possible because if the fire started in the lounge, as he said, then the

51

arsonists knew he wasn't in the house. So he said that he knew too much, that they were after his valuables. I got interested then. He's always snooping; he talks about "watchers" and no wonder: he's always watching people himself! I suggested he might have seen something he shouldn't, and he knew what I meant all right.'

'This has nothing to do with blackmail.' Miss Pink was firm. 'He hasn't got the confidence for it. He's pretending he holds files; he could have compiled some, but you may be sure they have no more relation to reality than the rest of his fantasy.'

Knox regarded the splintered door thoughtfully. 'People could think he was keeping tabs on them.'

'It's a harmless game.' Miss Pink was vehement. 'A secret life that started probably when he was adolescent and never grew out of.'

'His wife didn't think it was a game.'

'I don't like to see families broken up: children without a father and so on.'

Colour rose under the fair skin. He had a nervous mannerism of sucking in his cheeks. He was doing it now. 'Well, I've done all I mean to do here,' he said. 'I told him I'd have a look round, but I'll point out there wasn't much I could do without him here to let me in and see inside that lounge.' He shook his head. 'I'm a bit confused. I know he's mad, but is he sane enough to know I'm humouring him? Is he stringing me along? What would he do if I told him to forget the arsonist story and find some other way of getting his wife back?'

'Go along with the fantasy for the time being,' Miss Pink advised. 'If he pushes too hard, if he tries to embarrass you, you could make a casual mention of bringing in the CID. Of course, there shouldn't be any witnesses.'

She drove to Feartag to deliver the items she'd bought in Inverness. Beatrice had good news; she had convinced the Millars that the best thing they could do for Alec was to send him away for a month. The waiting list for state institutions was long, but she had found a place for him in a private holiday home. When Miss Pink asked how the Millars could afford the cost, Beatrice became flustered and changed the subject. 'So what's your news?' she asked. 'Did you paint Inverness red?'

'But you had all the excitement! Or haven't you heard about the fire at Campbell's cottage?'

She hadn't and Miss Pink enlightened her with an account that included his visit to her cottage last night. Beatrice was appalled. 'But weren't you terrified? Knocking at your window like that, virtually forcing his way in!'

'I was frightened, but had he been dangerous, the best way to deal with him was to let him talk. He's harmless providing he's treated correctly. Even Knox realises that.'

'And now you've met Knox, do you see why that embarrassing trick was played on him? With the car?'

'Not in the circumstances, although he could be unpopular with the local lads. He's intelligent and well-mannered. Frankly I'm surprised. It's usually the deadbeats in a police force who fetch up in remote villages.'

'He's well-mannered with ladies.'

'It's pleasant to be given a handle when one is addressed. I haven't been called "ma'am" since I left Montana.' Miss Pink was on the defensive. 'Speaking of charmers,' she began, and blushed but ploughed on, 'I picked up Flora MacKenzie hitch-hiking to Inverness.'

Beatrice sighed. 'She does it in summer-time too, when there's no knowing whom she might pick up. Suppose she encountered a motor-cycle gang? It doesn't bear thinking about. I blame Coline; she's wrapped up in her books. As for Ranald, he's hopeless as a father; I always thought he married Coline less for her money than for the security of having someone to order his life. He's like an old dog who's found a family to take him in. He's treated a bit like an old dog too.' She paused and, with one of those tangential swings to which Miss Pink was becoming accustomed, she went on, 'They can't blame Hell's Angels for the fire at Campbell's cottage.'

'Who – oh, yes; Ranald thought they were responsible for the thefts from cars in the summer. Do you think Campbell set fire to his own place?'

'I'm afraid he's capable of anything, but only as it relates to himself. He's not a vandal; all his hostility is directed inwards. If only his doctor could persuade him to have therapy . . . but he's unpredictable. He might well suspect a conspiracy. He would be right, of course.'

'But only in order to help him.'

'Can he see the difference?'

When Miss Pink returned to her cottage, the front door was wide open. From upstairs came the whine of a vacuum cleaner. Mary MacLeod, a large cheerful woman in her fifties, was doing her weekly chores. They exchanged pleasantries for a few moments, Mary obviously expecting more and, not getting it, taking the initiative. 'There was no fire, was there?' Her eyes were sparkling. 'I see the poliss followed you, but you all come back soon enough.'

Miss Pink was vague. 'Can you have smoke without fire? Does Mr Campbell bother you?'

'Never! He's good entertainment. He's clever too; I always tell him he should write a book, and off he goes – "Ah, Mary, I'll write a book one day that'll make your hair stand on end!"'

'What would he be writing *about*?'

Mary laughed gustily. 'Depends on his mood. If he's happy it's the network: spies, sleepers, "a web of intrigue", he says, and we make guesses who the controller is – like the spider at the middle of the web, see. But if someone's annoyed him, then he drops hints about people in the village.'

'Doesn't that upset people?'

Mary shrugged. '"If the cap fits, wear it." But most people take it in good part. I mean, it's all fun, isn't it?'

She turned to her vacuum and Miss Pink retreated to the shore, where the birds were feeding on the ebb tide. She had been there only a few minutes when there was a crash of breaking china behind her. A cyclist swerved at an alarming angle and she winced as Hamish Knox fell heavily, scraping the tarmac. Above him in an upper window of the Post Office Alec Millar was poised, about to throw a large bowl.

'No, Alec!' Miss Pink shouted, starting to run.

There were people in the Post Office doorway, staring open-mouthed. The bowl emerged in a lazy curve and smashed beside Hamish, who rolled clear with his arms round his head.

Miss Pink reached him. Throwing a prudent glance upwards, she saw an empty window space and heard Rose Millar's raised voice. She knelt beside Hamish who sat up, white and gasping, straightening one leg, then the other. Ranald MacKay emerged from the Post Office. Behind him Duncan Millar hovered in the doorway. Broken china was strewn across the roadway.

'I'd better get out of here,' Hamish muttered. 'Look at my bike!' He was obviously frightened.

'Can you stand?' Miss Pink asked.

'What happened?' Ranald blustered. 'There was this crash and the boy knocked off his cycle – did someone throw something?' He glared at the littered road.

Hamish was standing, trying to grin. 'That's the second time in two days—' He glanced at the open window. At that moment it was slammed down by Rose, who avoided looking at the group below.

'Let's go home and get you cleaned up,' Miss Pink said. 'Ranald, move his bike to the side.'

'I'll bring it,' Ranald said gallantly, but the front wheel was out of alignment and he had to hoist the machine on his shoulder.

'Very well, me boy' – he was taking charge – 'I'll go ahead and warn your mother, tell her to put the kettle on.'

'She's cleaning up at the lodge,' Hamish told him. 'I'm in luck,' he said to Miss Pink. 'She'd have a fit if she saw me like this.' His smile was like his father's. 'She treats me as if I was six years old.'

'You've certainly been in the wars recently. What on earth did Alec throw at you?'

'*Alec?*' Ranald turned so sharply that Miss Pink had to dodge the bicycle. 'Alec threw that china?'

'It came from the room above the shop.'

'It was Alec all right.' Hamish was gloomy. 'He's after my blood.'

'Ah!' Ranald remembered. 'You killed that wretched lapdog. Couldn't stand the thing meself: neurotic, yappy little runt. A good move, me boy.'

'I didn't do it deliberately,' Hamish protested.

'Of course not. The result's the same for all that. Now where shall I put this bike?'

'Anywhere; it doesn't matter so long as Dad doesn't run over it when he comes home. You going, sir? Thanks for helping.'

'Sure you're all right? You've got Miss Pink there to take care of you. 'Morning to you, ma'am.'

He tipped the brim of his deerstalker and strode down the drive from the police house. Miss Pink opened the side door and they went in, the boy looking at his hands in consternation. Blood was encrusted with dirt and sand. He led the way to the kitchen.

'Nurse Wallace—' Miss Pink began.

'Miss!' Hamish was indignant. 'I'm sixteen! I fell off my bike. I'm all *right*! Please, if you'd just run the water for me.'

She grunted. 'I daresay you're healthy enough to resist infection.' She ran the water lukewarm and stood back, gritting her teeth when he cringed as he sluiced his hands.

He told her where to find the first-aid kit in the office. She bandaged his hands, but he said his knees were all right; he'd fallen on his hip. 'The other one this time.'

She made a pot of tea and they sat at the kitchen table.

'We nearly met three days ago,' she said meaningly. 'On the shore.'

'I was keeping an eye on you – because you were with Campbell. He's mad; he set fire to his own house.'

'You don't think I can take care of myself?'

'My dad says you're a magistrate, but I don't think that makes a lot of difference. You know the law, but you can't know how Campbell's mind works. Can you tell me why he says he's working for the Special Branch?'

'Did you never dream of being something exciting: a pop star or a fighter pilot?'

'I did, but I grew out of it.'

'Campbell didn't grow out of it.'

'You mean he's retarded?'

'Only where his ambitions are concerned.'

'It colours everything he does.'

'You sound hostile.'

'I'll say I'm hostile. He scares me stiff! And all the other lads in the village. You never know what he'll do next.'

'Some of your friends have guilty consciences.'

'No. Well, not exactly. But sometimes, just now and again, you know, someone's old man might – I say *might* – have taken his lad on a fishing trip and maybe a fish was in the wrong place at the right time. I think that kind of thing might have happened.' He eyed her anxiously.

'Hamish, the occasional salmon doesn't give Campbell a hold over anyone. Besides, how would he know?'

'He's supposed to have night glasses; he knows all the surveillance techniques. He keeps records. That's why he's unpopular.'

'I didn't know he was.'

'My dad says he's got files.'

'If I was writing a book about this area, I'd keep files. Would that bother people?'

He grinned. 'Depends what was in 'em.'

'Skeletons in the closet? People with guilty consciences have to live with them, but I'll tell you this for what it's worth: no one with a conscience will make a successful criminal, so poaching and practical jokes are counter-productive.'

'I haven't done any poaching.' His eyes were guileless. 'But talking about a conscience, I do feel bad about Alec's dog.'

'You'll have to keep out of his way for a while. If that bowl had landed on your head, it could have meant a fractured skull.'

'He'd kill me if he got a chance.'

'Keep out of his way. You can't afford another confrontation because he might have a stroke, and that could be fatal. Then you'd feel more guilty still.'

'Oh Lord!'

A form passed the kitchen window. A door opened and a thin dark woman hurried in, dropped her shopping bag, checked at sight of Miss Pink, and was mesmerised by the bandages on Hamish's hands.

'Are you all right, son?'

'Mum! This lady's Miss Pink. She bandaged my hands. I fell off my bike, that's all.'

Wide, strained eyes fastened on Miss Pink. 'Sorry, miss. Did you bring him home? Thank you. Did you make tea for him? That was kind of you. Is there . . . ' She faltered, as if trying to think of the correct form of recompense.

'I didn't do anything,' Miss Pink said. 'Hamish cleaned his own—'

'That Alec Millar!' Mrs Knox wasn't listening. 'He could have killed you. Sir Ranald told me; I met him on his way back to the lodge. Said that Alec threw a pitcher and bowl out of the bedroom window.'

'Well, he didn't throw the potty, Mum.'

'Hush! In front of this lady!'

Miss Pink stood up, but she wasn't allowed to slip away. Mrs Knox accompanied her out to the drive, reiterating her gratitude until she remembered her boy was alone and unattended in the kitchen and flew back to comfort him. Poor lad, Miss Pink thought, it's fortunate he has a good father – and then wondered why she should think Gordon Knox good.

As she turned into the street, she met Esme Dunlop carrying something in a paper bag.

"Morning. Anything broken?' Esme's eyes were on the police house.

'No, only grazes. Where were you?'

'In my living room. I heard a noise and there you were, all converging on Hamish. I've brought him some fruit.'

'He won't thank you for it.' Miss Pink was grimly amused, then she softened. 'I mean, there's his mother about to wrap him in swaddling clothes. I think fruit from another woman might be salt in the wound. He has his dignity.'

'Has he?' It was tart. 'You could be right.' Esme turned and fell into step. After a moment she said, 'I hear Campbell's house caught fire.'

'Just a small fire in the living room. I think Mr Knox has everything under control.'

'I suppose Campbell did start it.'

Miss Pink shrugged. 'I'm a stranger in Paradise.'

Esme looked at her sharply. 'Oh, I see. Very neat, yes.'

They came to the Post Office. Miss Pink kept walking. 'I have to do my shopping,' Esme said, and slipped inside. She was reluctant to talk – and that was out of character. The mail box, set in the window, reminded Miss Pink of that letter with its message composed of words cut from newspapers. That was yesterday morning. Twenty-four hours seemed a long time for a person like Esme to be subdued.

Chapter 6

A crimson Mercedes swept up the street and stopped as Miss Pink reached her cottage. Coline stepped out, stylish in designer jeans and tooled Western boots.

'Do you mind if we talk, Melinda – I can call you that? It's by way of being important.'

They went indoors, Miss Pink brought out the sherry and Coline came straight to the point. 'What's this about the business of the keeper's cottage: the fire, so-called?'

'I don't know enough about it to reach a conclusion.'

'Oh, come on! You were there this morning; Knox told me. And Campbell says you agreed that it was arsonists.'

Miss Pink looked pained. 'Campbell came here last night and talked. You don't tell a man in his condition that the arsonists exist only in his imagination, and imply that he set the fire himself. I didn't know that there *was* a fire, so I went up this morning to find out.'

Coline nodded briskly. 'He set some furniture alight. Two armchairs are a write-off, and the sofa; we can never clean the soot off. The rest of the room he'll have to deal with himself. He'll do it; I've had a heart-to-heart talk with him. I went along with the arsonist theory too; he wouldn't have agreed to redecorate otherwise. We can replace the furniture easily enough – our attics are full of junk; but he'll have to live in an unfurnished parlour for a while: teach him a lesson.'

'I doubt that. You wouldn't think therapy more appropriate?'

'A psychiatrist? Who's to persuade him? He's all right this morning; he came up to the lodge early, very contrite. He said it was "them", a kind of ritual accusation, you know? But he was really apologising for the mess. I hope Debbie comes back soon. It's all her fault, silly woman.'

Miss Pink looked doubtful. 'So we all go along with the fantasies. Don't you think it's possible that our collusion could be making him worse – driving him to greater lengths in order to attract attention? I do feel that this kind of behaviour is a cry for help.'

Coline regarded her with interest. 'You're more familiar with this kind of thing than I am. All right, I'll have a word with his doctor when I get home. I might give Anne Wallace a ring too. I have to go to the shop now and ask after Alec. What a ridiculous thing to happen! It would be a poodle, wouldn't it? Any dog with a grain of sense would have frozen when it saw a horse coming fast. Apparently this thing ran straight into the pony. This is a good fino – Tio Pepe? You must have brought your wines with you.'

'I was in Inverness yesterday. I picked Flora up on the Lamentation Road.'

'How you do roll that out – but it is an exquisite name. Kind of you to give her a lift.'

'I took her as far as Inverness; she said she'd catch the train from there.'

'I doubt if she did that, she'd rather have the money. Once you were out of sight she'd have continued hitching to Edinburgh.'

'She told me she's interested in writing.'

Coline was mildly surprised. 'You could have fooled me.'

'People tell strangers things they'd never mention to their families. We discussed writing as a career and she was intrigued by the idea of journalism.'

'Was she now? And you volunteered to test the water. Well, I see no reason why she shouldn't go to some college of journalism, or whatever. How on earth does one teach people to write? I picked it up, as I assume you did. However, a college would keep her out of mischief until she marries. Oh, there's Esme. Esme!'

Esme Dunlop, hurrying past the open door, turned back at the call.

'Come and have a glass of sherry,' Miss Pink said, getting up for another glass. The woman entered carefully, like a nervous dog.

'Can you come up this afternoon?' Coline asked. 'I had a call from Timothy – my agent,' she explained to Miss Pink. 'The ending of *Orient* is ambivalent, Esme; we have to tighten it. That means the last two chapters must be rewritten. Come back with me now and we'll have a bite to eat and get stuck into it.'

Esme plucked her lip. 'Fine,' she said, without enthusiasm. 'I'll do that.' She accepted a sherry from Miss Pink and drank absently.

'Something wrong?' Coline asked, showing her annoyance. 'You've made other plans?'

Esme started. 'Oh, no, it's quite convenient. I'm not doing anything—' She stopped short.

'So?'

'Nothing.' The tone was surly. Coline stared at her and the silence was intimidating. 'I had a letter,' Esme said.

'What kind of letter?'

'Can't you guess? We all deal with fiction, don't we?' It was hurled at them.

Coline looked bewildered. 'Anonymous?' Miss Pink asked.

'You saw it,' Esme said.

'I glimpsed the type – I mean the format. The words were probably cut from newspaper headlines.'

Now Coline was fascinated. 'What did it say?'

'I'm not going to tell you. It was disgusting and it was a lie. No one is going to know – well, he knows, the one who sent it, but—'

'"He"?' Coline and Miss Pink spoke together.

'You know who sent it?' Coline pressed.

'I know.' Her expression was defiant.

After a moment Coline said, 'I wouldn't think you had an enemy in the village. Who've you been rubbing up the wrong way?'

'I haven't. It's evil, that's what it is – like random violence, only this is random torture.'

Coline laughed. 'Ignore it! You said it wasn't true. I've been getting this kind of thing ever since I started to get my name in the papers. You know I do.' She addressed Miss Pink: 'She filters my mail, but occasionally she tells me she burns a letter.' She turned back to Esme. 'Isn't that right?'

'It's my job to monitor your fan mail – we discussed that when you interviewed me for the position. It makes a hell of a lot of difference when the message is intended for yourself.'

'Was it a local postmark?' Miss Pink asked.

'This is my problem. I'm going to deal with it.'

'Look,' Coline was earnest, 'you're accused of some crime – or sin, or whatever some diseased mind thinks is a perversion, and you know it's a lie, so the whole thing is ridiculous. Forget it. Or give the thing to me, and the name of the sender, and I promise you he'll never send another poison pen letter after I've had a session with him.'

'The same applies to me,' Esme said coldly, 'so let's leave it, shall we? I assure you I can cope. I'll nip over and lock my door and then I'll come up to the lodge, right?'

'How bizarre,' Coline exclaimed, scarcely giving the woman time to get out of earshot. 'Do you believe her?'

'She certainly had a letter. As for whether she knows the identity of the sender, that's a different matter. She's implying it's a local person, of course.'

'Sometimes people send letters to themselves,' Coline said darkly.

'You've known her for a long time. She's insecure, but she hasn't given me the impression of being that unbalanced. On the contrary, I'd say she's got all her wits about her; she's just short on judgement of other people's feelings.'

'Quite. Like I said, she's rubbed someone up the wrong way. She rolls right over people, and she's got a hide like a rhinoceros. She dominates Ranald, but then he wants to be dominated. Flora keeps out of her way for the most part, and as for me, I allow her to run the secretarial side – she's good at that – but when it comes to my personal life, that's a no-go area.'

'And how do you draw the line?'

'A broad hint that she's being rather too masculine, dear.'

'I think you've guessed what was in that letter.'

Coline smiled thinly. 'I've no sympathy for the woman. There's nothing wrong with her; she's just self-indulgent. She's got plenty of control for most of the time; she has to learn to assert it all the time and stop trying to run other people's lives.'

When Coline left Miss Pink closed her front door, not wanting more visitors as she prepared the meal she was to serve Beatrice. The afternoon was still and beautiful. Sunshine slanted across the loch and for a short time flooded the sitting room. The front window was open and she was vaguely conscious of sounds: of gulls and curlews, sandpipers and oystercatchers, and an outboard motor. A car passed occasionally. At one point there was shooting from the direction of the North Wood: different types of weapon; Beatrice must be firing her brother's guns.

By tea-time the kitchen was a confusion of dishes in different stages of preparation, of food scraps and spilled packets – and a sink so packed with dirty dishes that the surplus was stacked on the floor.

With the oven going full blast, she opened the back window. The garden was in shade, but the escarpment and the trees were in brilliant sunlight. The rock glowed pink, grass was emerald, foliage was touched with garnet and gold. She sipped cooking burgundy from a measuring jug and contemplated the skyline which, unknown for a time, was now known. She hoped that the fact that she derived pleasure from having been on a cliff a few hundred feet high instead of a peak of several thousand feet was not a sign of decrepitude. She looked back at her kitchen, deploring its domesticity, never realising that it was as un-domesticated as a gangland squat.

Her eyes returned to the escarpment, but she caught a movement much closer at hand. The plots at the backs of the houses were bounded by an old stone wall. The park's timber came right up to this so that, with the fruit trees in the paddocks and hawthorns along the wall, the cover extended almost to the houses. But here and there a section of the wall could be glimpsed, at this hour floodlit by the sinking sun. She had seen something move on the other side of the wall and now a figure appeared on top, jumped lightly to the ground and disappeared. She thought she recognised Hamish Knox, which wasn't surprising; Mary MacLeod lived on the far side of the Post Office, then came the police house. Evidently Hamish had been up to the lodge, probably to exercise the ponies. He wouldn't want to go along the street and up the lodge drive, because that would take him past the front of the Post Office. In any event, with his bicycle unusable this back way would be the quickest. She applauded his good sense – and was galvanised into activity as she realised that a second batch of cheese straws was burning.

The smell was still hanging about when Beatrice arrived at seven o'clock. Miss Pink apologised and, with the sherry, served potato crisps hurriedly purchased at the Post Office. They discussed Alec, Beatrice having heard about the morning's incident from Greg Sinclair, the widower from the old schoolhouse who kept bees and had brought her some honey. 'That was the excuse,' she said. 'The real reason was to find out what I knew about the confrontation between Alec and Hamish. My not knowing it had taken place was a bonus for the old fellow. How is Hamish?'

'He was a bit shaken up.' Miss Pink threw a calculating glance towards the kitchen and relaxed enough to take a few sips of sherry. 'I find it hard to believe that he had a hand in that trick with his father's car. He appears a normal youth: innocent, naive. . . . Why should he want to embarrass his father?'

'Jealousy?'

'Of Anne Wallace?'

'No. Of his father's *machismo*. During the season young girls, particularly foreigners, flock round him. And then there's the flouting of authority; in this case rebellious youth gets his father and the police in one fell swoop.'

'You've given this some thought. Have you worked out who is writing the anonymous letters?'

'Gracious! Who's receiving them?'

Miss Pink related Esme Dunlop's experience and Beatrice looked grave. 'I don't like it; it's disturbing. It's not the same thing, is it? Like the unpleasant telephone calls, an anonymous letter's in a different category from a practical joke with a car.'

'An escalation of mischief?' Miss Pink stood up and Beatrice followed her to the kitchen. She surveyed the clutter and said absently, 'Campbell's not himself either.'

'I'm not sure what his natural self is, but how is he deviating?'

'He's tense – as if he were on drugs, but I don't think he takes them. He's been at the house this afternoon, getting the last of the logs under cover and helping me clean the guns.'

'I heard the firing. Let's hope the heavy breather did too. People know now that you're not as vulnerable as you appear to be.'

There seemed to be a tacit agreement to keep the conversation light while they were eating. So with the baked scallops Beatrice expounded on the magic of fishing for sea trout, and with the veal olives Miss Pink reciprocated with the joys of desert travel. They demolished an extravagent *torta di noti*, followed by a reasonable piece of Stilton and then, having cleared the table, they sat by the fire, coffee and brandy between them.

At nine o'clock there was a sound of skidding tyres in the street and someone thudded on the front door. It was no knock but a hammering with the clenched fist. They stared at each other in astonishment. Miss Pink got to her feet. 'Who is it?' she called.

'Campbell. Can I speak to you, miss?'

Beatrice came and stood beside her. 'I'm here too, Campbell: Miss Swan. Are you drunk?'

'No, Miss Swan. I'm glad you're there; I want to see you too.'

Beatrice pushed past Miss Pink and opened the door. Campbell entered wide-eyed, removing his cap. 'They set my place afire,' he said.

They turned away from him. 'Sit down, Campbell,' Miss Pink said comfortably. 'You'll take a whisky?' She bit her lip to keep from smiling. To have offered him brandy would have seemed like a slavish imitation of last night.

'I can't stop,' he said, 'but I'll take a dram.'

Beatrice was watching him. 'Is the fire bad?'

He nodded. 'They've finished the place this time. Thank God no one was inside.'

'It's Lady MacKay's property.' It was a gentle rebuke.

'She says it's insured. Miss Swan, let me have one of the guns.'

'Whatever for?'

'I need protection. I can smell petrol at that place. They would have thought I was inside. When they know I didn't die in the fire, they'll come after me.'

'No, Campbell; I'm not lending you a gun.'

'Miss, I got to have protection!' His voice was rising.

'Campbell!' Miss Pink spoke loudly. 'Why did they set fire to your house two nights running? You were here only last night.'

'That's right, I was.' He seemed surprised. 'This is different. I know why this happened. I'll tell you. I should have told you first, but I was shocked. It's not nice to come home and see your place blazing.'

'You've called the fire brigade?'

He gave a snort of derision. 'Fire brigade's in *Morvern*! But if it was here, in Sgoradale, it wouldn't be no good. The place is destroyed, and all my belongings. Hell, who cares? I'm worried about my *life* now. What happened? I come back from Miss Swan's this afternoon and I find them in my house, one of them anyway; maybe the other got out when they heard the sound of the van. Last one couldn't get out because I've nailed up the back door, so the only way out is the front door, see? And they'd forced that. The crowbar they'd used was there on the step – taken from my own barn. So I knew the place had been broke into – again, but I never thought anyone was still there. He must have been hiding in the lounge. I went in the kitchen and he hit me from behind. Knocked me down, but didn't make me unconscious. When I picked myself up he was away. I run outside and he's streaking for the trees like a deer. I couldn't have caught him; he was much too fast.'

'Who was he?' Beatrice asked.

'He was wearing a hood. And jeans and a dark anorak.'

'But the place wasn't on fire then,' Miss Pink said.

'No, not then. I hung around waiting for him to come back but he didn't, so I went down the bar. The men there told me to fingerprint the place. I'd do that anyway; he hadn't been wearing gloves. I stayed in the bar too long. When I went home again the place was afire. He'd come back to destroy his prints.'

Beatrice sighed and Miss Pink said, 'Are you saying he slipped out of the bar, set the place on fire and came back?'

'I hadn't thought of that. It's possible, but I shouldn't think it's likely. I'd have noticed he'd gone away. No, what happened was when I was chasing him earlier, when he ran out of the cottage and I saw him making for the trees, I shouted after him, "I've got you now: you left your prints." He had to have come back when I was down the bar. Now, Miss Swan, will you let me have a gun? Doesn't have to be a rifle. Shotgun will do.'

'No, Campbell. Now you go home—'

'You weren't listening! I got no home! It's been burned—'

'Campbell!' Again Miss Pink tried to stem the flood. 'What was he doing in your place the first time, before he set it on fire?'

He shrugged angrily. 'I don't know. Looking for something. The place had been burglarised: all the drawers pulled out, books on the floor. Doesn't matter about that; they're after me now. I'm not sleeping in this village tonight. I'm a marked man. I'm getting out now.' And he went, closing the door quietly. They sat looking at each other.

'He hasn't taken his van,' Miss Pink said.

Beatrice pointed to the window. 'Listening,' she mouthed.

'It's a very strange story,' Miss Pink said loudly.

'I'm going to telephone Knox.' Beatrice went to the telephone and held a one-sided conversation with a non-existent police station. She replaced the receiver. 'He's on his way,' she said.

After a few moments they opened the front door. Campbell's van stood there, lit by the street lamp.

'He's not in it,' Beatrice said.

Miss Pink found a torch and shone it inside the van. 'Just another move in the game,' she said in exasperation.

'Oh, God!' Beatrice breathed. 'Look!' Her fingers dug into Miss Pink's arm.

There was a glow above the Lamentation Road and the rocks of the escarpment leapt and faded in a pink light against which the trees were clearly silhouetted. Smoke billowed and rolled upwards. Golden sparks flew like fireflies.

Then they did ring Knox.

Chapter 7

People converged on the burning cottage. Gordon Knox was followed by Miss Pink and Beatrice. They left the Renault in the car park; the fire brigade would need a clear run to the cottage – although by the time it arrived there would be little left to do but damp down the embers. When they walked up the short track, they saw that already the roof had fallen in and only a few rafters were left flaming against the smoke. The fire still raged inside the walls: a glimpse of hell through the angular voids which had been windows and a front door.

'I'm relieved that no one was inside,' Miss Pink observed, 'but it's still sad to think of the lives that were lived out here: people who loved the place and were happy in it. As if the ghosts had lost their home.'

'*He* wasn't happy,' Beatrice said. 'That's why he burned it.'

'He must have been happy here in the early days, and with a young family. All the more reason for destroying it – to emphasise his present misery. He swings to extremes.'

Beatrice turned away. 'It's unbearable, like suicide. Where do you think he is now?'

'I've no idea. Here's Knox. Where have you been, Mr Knox?'

He was in gumboots and anorak, and he carried a heavy torch. 'I was in the barn. There's a stink of petrol but no sign of fire in there. The man's mad. I don't know what Lady Coline's going to say. This could be her now.'

Two sets of headlights were approaching through the trees, diminished by the glare. When they stopped people came stumbling forward, bobbing in front of the lamps until the firelight revealed them as a group of men – some a little unsteady on their feet.

'Customers from the bar,' Knox said drily.

The newcomers pushed forward, Duncan Millar and Sinclair,

69

the apiarist, in front. The old men regarded the burning cottage in silence, while from behind them came a murmur ranging from incredulity to grim humour. That last would be the younger men, Miss Pink thought.

'Has anyone seen Campbell?' Knox asked.

'He can't be inside!' someone said.

'No, there's no one inside. Campbell's been in the village since it started.'

'He's been—' There was a swift movement in the gloom and the words were choked off.

'He was in the bar,' Duncan Millar said firmly.

'What time?' asked Knox. 'What time did he come in?'

'Seven, maybe.'

'Nearer seven-thirty,' Sinclair said.

'What time did he leave?'

The old men looked at each other. 'Nine?' Sinclair suggested. 'Round about then.'

'It was nine o'clock when he called on us,' Miss Pink said. They had told Knox on the telephone that they'd seen Campbell since the fire was started, but had had no time to tell him more, except that they didn't know the man's present whereabouts. 'He said the place was on fire then,' she reminded him.

'You phoned me at nine-forty, ma'am!'

'We didn't believe him,' Beatrice said, and the men muttered amongst themselves; they wouldn't have believed him either.

'Didn't he give any hint as to where he was going?' Knox asked wearily.

'No.' While Miss Pink was considering whether to add that Campbell had said he wouldn't sleep in the village, she saw more lights approaching. She decided to say nothing at this point and then realised from her silence that Beatrice had come to the same decision.

The new arrivals were Coline and Ranald. The men made way for them. Ranald was vociferously appalled, Coline mutely horrified. When Knox assured them that no one had been inside the cottage they were bewildered for a moment, trying to adjust to the mere destruction of property rather than loss of life.

70

'Well,' Coline breathed. 'Thank God for that!'

'Definitely,' echoed Ranald. 'Quite. Only bricks and mortar, what?'

Coline turned her back on the customers from the bar and addressed Miss Pink quietly. 'Where is he?'

'No one knows. He visited us, said the place was on fire, and we didn't believe him. Then he vanished.'

'And he said other people were responsible for the fire, of course.'

'He did.'

'I wonder—' Coline began, to be interrupted by Anne Wallace who had arrived unnoticed and pushed through the crowd of men. 'Is anyone hurt?' she asked urgently.

'Oh, Anne!' Coline greeted her with a kind of relief. 'He's done it again. You see! No, no, there's no one inside. We've talked on the phone,' she explained to Miss Pink. 'It's out of our hands now, Anne,' she said meaningly. 'This is a crime, isn't it, Knox?' She lowered her voice further, addressing the women. 'I shall use blackmail: we won't bring a charge provided he submits himself for treatment. How would that be?'

'I can't think of anything better at the moment,' Beatrice said. 'But no one's at their best for making an objective assessment. I shall go home now. I'm very sorry about your little house, Coline, my dear.'

'Thank you. I suppose we shall rebuild with the insurance money, so we'll be better off in the long run. All these old places are damp.'

As Miss Pink and Beatrice reached the street, an unearthly wail rent the night. Miss Pink switched off the engine and opened her door.

'It's the fire engine,' she said. 'They must be trying to move the sheep off the road. As Campbell said, a fire brigade fifteen miles away is no use in an emergency.'

They got out of the car and stood on the turf looking down the loch.

'Where do you think he went?' Miss Pink asked.

'A bothy back on the moors perhaps, or the woods . . . '

'What on earth's happened?' Esme had come silently across the grass from her house. 'I heard a siren. Is someone hurt?'

Beatrice gave her the gist of the night's happenings.

'So where is he now?' Esme asked. 'His van's still here; he can't go far without transport.' The van was where he had left it outside Miss Pink's front door.

'He has his boat,' Miss Pink said.

'He hasn't taken that anywhere. I've been reading this evening; I didn't have the television on, so I'd have heard the sound of an outboard. For my money, he's gone to ground with one of the crofters out on the lighthouse road.'

They looked at the few lights burning seaward of the North Wood. 'At least, I hope he has,' Esme said.

The search for Campbell started after breakfast. Coline was maintaining there was no proof that the cottage had been deliberately set on fire, and since the firemen confirmed that there were no human remains in the debris, word had gone out from the lodge that the fire was an accident. Nevertheless, some people felt a compulsion to find Campbell.

Knox was not on duty this weekend and, with Coline and Hamish on ponies and Ranald in a Land Rover, the four of them started to search. Miss Pink, rising late, went back to the ruins of the cottage.

No smoke rose from the charred remains inside the walls. Mindful of the danger to woodland, and of Coline's presence, the firemen had made a thorough job of damping down. Miss Pink stood in the gap where the front door had been and surveyed the interior. There was the shape of a blackened cooker, the metal struts and springs of three bedsteads, the frame of a table and what had been kitchen chairs. Everything that could burn had burned. The blaze had been intense.

She crossed a patch of grass where a sooty washing-line was stretched between a stout post and the barn. The latter was small, with half-doors in front and an ordinary door at the side which was open; it revealed a space which had once been a byre but was now used for storage. Driftwood was stacked against a wall above a saw-horse and chopping block. There was a work bench below a rack of tools. Everything was in good order and neatly hung or stacked: a cross-cut and a bow saw, a felling axe and hatchets, lobster pots, gardening implements. There were also two ten-gallon drums, one empty, the other indicating by its residue that it contained heavy oil. A five-gallon jerry-can lay empty on the earth floor. A dark patch reeked of petrol.

Miss Pink picked up a garden fork and returned to the cottage. Starting at the front door, she began to rake through the ashes, a task complicated by metal objects which had been contorted and fused: a heater, many small and unidentifiable structures and a curiously familiar article that turned out to be the keys and guts of a typewriter. The petrol smell was here too. There was a lot of glass where you'd expect to find it, under the window gaps. It crackled underfoot, but when she trod on something that rolled and didn't crack, she stopped and teased it clear with the fork.

First testing its temperature with a finger, she picked it up gingerly: a rounded piece of thick glass, black but still recognisable: part of a milk bottle.

She replaced the fork in the barn and started to search the old byre. In a manger she found a funnel. Leaving it where it was, she returned to her car and drove to Feartag.

'Petrol bombs?' exclaimed Beatrice, turning the piece of glass in her hand. 'I can't believe it! This could have come from a bottle that never contained anything other than milk.'

'True. But the petrol can has been emptied recently, and the funnel was used; there's a damp patch in the manger where it was lying. Certainly I can't think why he didn't carry the can to the cottage and splash the petrol around and set fire to a trail with a match. But if he'd done that, he'd surely have left the can at the fire, not replaced it in the barn. And where would the funnel come in? The way things are, it points to petrol bombs.'

'But you're implying – no, it's impossible.' Miss Pink was silent. Beatrice, watching her, said slowly, 'It looks as if he went to amazing lengths to try to prove someone was after him.'

Still Miss Pink said nothing. 'Who would hate him so much?' Beatrice asked weakly. 'You *are* suggesting that someone thought he was inside, or have I misread you completely?'

'Only partially. I wasn't thinking of a potential murderer, only an arsonist.'

'*Only?*'

'It's not so bad if the person didn't intend to kill Campbell, only to destroy fingerprints.'

'You've started to believe that story?'

'What time did Campbell leave here yesterday afternoon?'

'He finished at five. Why?'

'Some time around then, while the sun was still high enough to be on the wall at the back of the street, Hamish Knox came home the back way, through the park. I thought he'd been up at the lodge exercising the ponies.' Miss Pink moved across the sitting room and regarded the yellowing birches on the far bank of the river.

From behind her came a shocked voice: 'You're suggesting that Hamish had something to do with the fire?'

'What I'm saying is that it looks as if bottles were filled with petrol, that I can't think why Campbell should do that unless, as you say, he's trying to put the blame on someone else – and I'm telling you that I saw Hamish come home, and not openly, about the time when Campbell says he found an intruder in his cottage.'

'That's fantasy. Hamish would never break into a place, let alone set it on fire. Why should he? You're talking about mindless violence, the kind of thing you get in inner cities. I know these people. That cottage is Coline's property and she's well respected. And Hamish's father is the policeman!'

'Having an affair with the nurse.' Miss Pink tried to restore balance.

Beatrice shifted ground, but angrily. 'Have you forgotten Alec's dog? Hamish is guilty and terrified. I'd *expect* him to come home over his back wall; I'd be surprised if he didn't after what happened last time he went along the street. If anyone is dangerous in this village it's Alec, but that danger is out in the open. Of course,' she added more thoughtfully, 'Campbell is a danger to himself. Forget about Hamish. I feel I should be doing something. What do you say to taking a flask and some sandwiches and driving around?'

'Doing what?'

'Looking for Campbell, of course. I can't work in the garden knowing he's out there somewhere in need of help. And where's his boat anyway?'

'I've looked for it, but I can't see it anywhere in the bay.'

'Then let's start moving.'

They drove to the end of the lighthouse road where they found the lodge's Land Rover parked outside the perimeter wall. The light was automatic, so there were no keepers to call on. They walked down one side of the wall to the top of the cliffs, but saw nothing untoward except a group of gannets beating low past the headland. Beyond the Minch the hills of the Hebrides were insubstantial, a gauzy mirage.

Miss Pink sniffed the air. 'The wind's backing.'

Beatrice squinted at the Long Island. 'You're right, and the visibility's not so sharp. I think we've seen the last of the Indian summer.'

'Two more days, do you reckon?'

'Quite. This is a slow deterioration. Look at the sky.'

There were a few small clouds above the Hebrides, more to the east on the mainland mountains, but the sky was still blue, although robin's egg rather than gentian. As yet there was little to presage a break except for that hint of humidity in the west.

'Time enough to find him,' Miss Pink murmured. 'He can't have gone far.'

They turned and trudged up the slope. When they reached the road they looked towards the village, but it was hidden by the lie of the land and all they could see was an empty stretch of water and the wooded southern shore of the loch.

'I didn't realise how many trees there were on that side,' Miss Pink said. 'There should be pine martens.'

'That's not the shore. It is wooded, but those trees are on the islands. They're covered with scrub birch.'

'Is that so? And yesterday he was out on the loch. I thought he was fishing, but he could have been transporting stores.'

'There are no buildings on the islands, no ruins. And the fire wasn't until after dark.'

'The first fire was the previous evening. It would be logical to sleep on an island if you wanted people – including your wife – to think you were in danger.'

'Searching all the islands would take ages; they're terribly overgrown. We used to picnic on them, and fish. Ah, here's Ranald.' He was approaching from the far side of the lighthouse boundary.

'Good morning, ladies. Any news?' They shook their heads. 'And nothing here,' he went on. 'Although I'd hardly expect him to hang around, as it were. It's just that I told them I'd come to the point and work back. I started with the cliffs under the light; it'd be a good clean way to do it – straight over the edge. He doesn't own a gun.'

They stared at him. 'What makes you so sure he killed himself?' Beatrice asked.

He blinked owlishly. 'Well, if he meant to do it he's done it already. Wouldn't you say so?'

'Yes, but—'

'I don't think there can be any doubt about it: we're looking for a body. Have you been inside?' He gestured at the lighthouse. 'Can't get in the light, of course, but I'll have a look round the outbuildings and the old living quarters, see if anyone's broken in.'

'We'll leave that to you,' Beatrice said. 'We thought we'd go out to the islands.'

'The islands?' He looked across the loch. 'That's possible, or he could have holed up in a bothy. I still think he opted for a cliff. I'm going to look in the bays along the coast here where stuff washes up.'

'He's enjoying it,' Beatrice exclaimed as they started back.

'Enjoying the drama?' Miss Pink suggested. 'A defence mechanism perhaps; he doesn't relate the situation to a real person.'

'I hope you're right. I'd hate to think he was a ghoul.'

'He's repressed.'

Beatrice stared at her profile. 'People are speaking their minds today. Is this what happens to ordinary men and women in the proximity of violence?'

'The circumstances are abnormal. And what's this?'

A horse was standing across the road, Coline in the saddle and waving them down. She approached the driver's side. 'Melinda, you're just the person I need – and Beatrice. I want you to come and look at something.'

'What?'

'I don't know – something very odd indeed. I want your opinion. Follow me.'

She set off at a canter along the grass verge and Miss Pink followed, exchanging speculations with Beatrice. When they came to the North Wood, Coline took a cart track that led diagonally down the slope towards the loch. Beatrice said, 'This leads to Camas Beag. It's a holiday place, one of the more luxurious ones. But Campbell can't be there or she'd have said.'

'Does she own all this land?'

'Clear to the point. Presumably the Northern Lights lease the lighthouse property, and a few of the crofters have bought their places, as we did, but the holiday cottages belong to Coline. Stop here.'

The track widened to a turning circle under the gable end of a house. Coline had dismounted and was waiting for them. She led the way to the back of the building which at first sight was unremarkable: a stone-paved yard with outhouses, a dustbin, drains, back door, windows. They were casement windows with small panes; one pane was broken and the casement unlatched. The room beyond was the kitchen.

'Have you been inside?' Miss Pink asked, peering at what she could see of the interior.

'Yes. He's not here, but I'd like you to take a look and see if you can spot anything significant. I'm not a criminologist.'

They walked round to the front door. 'You mean there's nothing missing?' Miss Pink asked as Coline inserted a key in the lock.

'Not that I can tell. Of course, there's nothing of value in a holiday place . . .'

A subjective opinion, thought Miss Pink as they stepped inside. Camas Beag was furnished with some good Victorian pieces and Liberty fabrics. There was a large colour television set, electric radiators, a range of kitchen gadgets, a telephone – all except the phone were portable and desirable.

They went upstairs. There were three bedrooms and a bathroom. The bath fittings were whiter than white, the bedrooms so neat that the pale carpets showed no sign of traffic since they were last vacuumed. The beds were made up with patchwork quilts tucked under pillows in the fashion of hotels, with hospital corners at the feet.

'All the same,' mused Miss Pink, following unspoken thoughts, 'did you look in the wardrobes?'

Coline was appalled. 'Oh, no! No, I didn't. Are you going to?'

'Of course. We're here now. And the window is broken. When did you come here last – or anyone else who had a right to be here? Who looks after the place?'

'Mary MacLeod. The last tenants left two weeks ago; Mary would have cleaned after they went and I doubt if she's been back since. I'll ask her.'

She went downstairs and Miss Pink walked from room to room opening wardrobes and cupboards, pulling out drawers – which were all empty – looking under beds.

'Surely no one's been up here,' Beatrice remarked, watching from a doorway.

'There's no sign of it, but someone broke in. Why?'

Below stairs Coline was talking on the telephone. They descended and Miss Pink went to the kitchen. She studied the stainless steel draining boards, the double sink, the white tiles of the window sill, stooping to look along the shining surfaces.

'If someone came in,' she said, 'they removed all their traces.'

Coline appeared in the doorway. 'Mary says she hasn't been back since she cleaned two weeks ago. The window wasn't broken then.'

'She has her own key?' Miss Pink asked.

'Yes, all the places have duplicate keys. The cleaners have one, I keep the other and hand mine to the tenants when they arrive.'

Miss Pink went to the sitting room. There were two main rooms downstairs; the second was a dining room. The others trailed after her. She turned to Coline. 'You think there's nothing missing, but didn't anything strike you as odd when you came in the first time, on your own?'

Coline shook her head helplessly. 'I came in the front way because the back door's bolted. Nothing seemed odd until I went to the kitchen and saw the window, then I thought that the weirdest thing was that there *was* nothing wrong. I mean, even the tinned food doesn't seem to have been touched. If it was Campbell or a tramp who broke in, then he didn't sleep or eat here. If it was a thief, he didn't steal anything. Surely a burglar would at least have taken the food mixer for his mother or his girl-friend.' She sounded affronted.

They went outside and she locked the front door. 'I've told Mary to send Sinclair to replace the pane,' she said. 'It's a mystery. Has it given you any ideas?'

Miss Pink shook her head. 'Not yet. Something may occur to me.'

Coline untied the pony's halter. 'What do you propose to do now?'

Beatrice said, 'We thought we'd borrow a dinghy and take a look at the islands.'

'That's a good idea. His boat isn't around. Damn, it's low tide and we'll never get our boat across the sand. I know – we'll take Sinclair's dinghy; it's on the bar below the schoolhouse. I'll see you there.' She mounted and pushed the pony down a slope so steep he was sliding on his haunches like a dog. They came out on a strip of sand and set off at a canter towards the village.

'I'm glad she's coming,' Beatrice said. 'She's happy with engines, I'm not.'

'She took it for granted that she should join us.'

'The islands are part of the estate. Nothing happens in Sgoradale without the family being concerned.'

At any other time exploring the southern shore would have been sheer delight; even today, searching for a man in trouble, they couldn't fail to be affected by the beauty of the islands. The water was calm and Coline had no difficulty in navigation. Even underwater reefs appeared innocuous as the boat slipped past submerged rocks and their fringes of waving weed.

From a distance the islands looked like a solid mass, but on approach miniature straits and channels revealed a maze of rock and water. In places Coline cut the engine and they pushed themselves along the rock with their hands. A seal bobbed up and followed them for a while like an inquisitive labrador. A heron gave an angry croak and flapped away, trailing water across the surface. On a patch of grass at the back of a small bay a group of barnacle geese was grazing. Some of the islands were several hundred yards in length and even the heather was tall enough to conceal a man if he were lying down; the trees would have hidden a tent.

'All the same,' Miss Pink said, 'he can't hide the boat. It's too heavy for one man to drag into the timber, and we've seen no caves.'

'There're none on the shore either,' Coline told her. 'The nearest caves are in the big cliffs under the lighthouse.'

'There's nothing for it. We have to go ashore.'

'But if his boat's not here—' Beatrice protested.

'He could have set it adrift or sunk it.'

'But that would mean—'

'Let's start with the islands in the middle,' Miss Pink said. 'Those most effectively concealed from the mainland.'

It was hot and exhausting work. The heather was full of dust and pollen, and a smell of old honey. Blackbirds fled from them shrieking, eider duck grumbled in the shallows and the three women ploughed doggedly through the undergrowth, more than one of them wondering if this were not a waste of time, merely a show of concern.

They shared their lunch with Coline, sitting on rock slabs across the water from the island where the barnacle geese were grazing. 'We'll try there next,' Miss Pink said.

The geese padded to the other side of the bay as the women trudged up the sand. On the higher ground there was gorse, then came rock outcrops with the heather and old gnarled birches rooted in the cracks. Miss Pink was in the lead when she stopped suddenly.

The camouflage was almost perfect. It was a dull green pup tent, its ridge descending almost to the ground, and it was closed.

'Campbell?' Miss Pink called, but no one responded, nothing moved. She unzipped the flysheet to reveal the tent proper, also fastened. She opened the second zip and the sides fell loose. The interior was a green gloom and it was untenanted. She sat back on her heels and the others peered over her shoulders.

The tent wasn't empty; there were possessions: a sleeping bag, a camping stove, a set of dixies and cutlery – clean and stacked – a few tins of food: beans, potatoes, stewed steak. Miss Pink backed out and rose to her feet. 'Now where did he go?'

They closed the tent and went back to the shore. She looked around and said, 'This bay is invisible except from the next island. He could come and go unseen by anyone on the mainland. He could take off down the loch and once he passed behind an island he could enter the maze and no one would· know where he was.'

'Who'd be interested?' Coline asked. 'No one̦ was after him. We agreed that was a fantasy.'

Beatrice said suddenly, 'I'm going to leave a note in the tent. He trusts me and he has no friends; he needs help and he knows I can supply it.'

They agreed that leaving a note could do no harm; it might flush him out, and he had to be located for his own good. Miss Pink found a pencil and they returned to the tent where Beatrice wrote a message on a label from a tin of beans and placed it on the groundsheet under the tin. As they retreated Coline asked what she'd written.

Beatrice said, 'I want both of you to keep this confidential. I promised him that no one else would be at the meeting and that I'd tell no one the location.'

'Do you think that's wise?' Coline asked.

'I've been employing him for ten years.'

Miss Pink said nothing. Later, in the boat, she mentioned the bothies on the moors and utilising horses to reach them; she considered her own participation, but thought the lodge ponies too small for her weight. Who did the exercising in Flora's absence, she asked casually; she'd seen someone riding yesterday – Hamish?

'That would be him,' Coline said. 'He comes up every day. He's paid, of course, but he has to groom and muck out and everything.'

Miss Pink felt old eyes watching her.

'Would you like me to keep you company this evening?' she asked, passing Beatrice the shortbread. They were drinking tea in Miss Pink's sitting room.

Knox had seen them coming in and was waiting below the schoolhouse when Coline put them ashore. They had come to the conclusion that there was no point in looking further for Campbell, at least until tomorrow, by which time it was hoped he would have approached Beatrice. There wasn't much they could do anyway; there were only two or three hours of daylight left. Hamish had ridden to the southern headland and he would come back before dark; Sir Ranald had given up and gone home saying that if Campbell were in hiding four people weren't going to find him, and if he was dead there was no urgency.

Coline took her pony out of Sinclair's paddock and rode back to the lodge, while Miss Pink took Beatrice home for tea and discussion.

'I'd prefer to be alone this evening,' Beatrice said. 'And I promised Campbell I wouldn't reveal the meeting place, remember? I feel I have to meet him on his own level. But I assure you I'll telephone as soon as he's gone, if possible.'

'If possible?'

'He may ask me to promise not to call anyone.'

'Then I shall call you.'

'Don't do that. An interruption could be fatal.'

'That's an unfortunate turn of phrase. But it's because he is so unpredictable that I feel some precautions should be taken.'

'If he intends harm, a telephone call isn't going to avert it.'

Miss Pink filled their cups and passed the milk. 'You have firearms.' It was a statement, not a question, but when her guest

82

didn't respond Miss Pink looked at her with deliberation.

Beatrice raised her eyes from her cup. 'Yes,' she said, without inflection. 'I have Robert's guns.'

'I'm wondering if you're doing the right thing.'

'He knows he has nothing to fear from me. He's simple, like an animal. I've always known how to deal with him, and we've never had a misunderstanding. Don't worry about it; I'm quite confident.'

She was adamant and Miss Pink made no further move to dissuade her from being alone when she met Campbell, if he came. Would he return to the tent, and would he accept the invitation if he did so? She pondered these questions when Beatrice had left, and wondered if much hinged on the outcome in any event. It was possible that he would leave his spartan camp, particularly if the weather broke, and return to the village without visiting Beatrice. He had no home, but his van was still outside the cottage. The keys had been in the ignition and Miss Pink had moved it to the verge across the road, close to her Renault where it wouldn't block her view of the loch. She had left the keys where they were.

The sun set, the afterglow lingered, darkness fell. She would have liked to go out and stand on the shore listening for the sound of oars. If he slept on the island last night and Esme heard no outboard motor, then he must have rowed there. By now, if his paranoia were rampant, he would have muffled the oars. But she didn't go outside; he would be watchful as a wild beast and she must leave the field to him and Beatrice. She drew her curtains and switched on the television.

The telephone rang while she was watching the ten o'clock news. She sighed with relief when she heard the familiar voice.

'I'm all right,' Beatrice said in answer to the inevitable question, sounding exasperated that it should have been asked. 'And *he*'s all right. No problems. He's coming ashore tomorrow and he's agreed to see his doctor on Monday. We'll keep this to ourselves, shall we? It embarrasses him. I have to call Coline and Knox, of course, but I shall say as little as possible to Knox.'

'Was Campbell amenable?'

'Oh, yes, I had no trouble with him at all. He's had a bad time. By the way, he'll be moving his van; don't be surprised when you hear the engine start. You left the keys in it, didn't you?'

'Yes. Where will he put it?'

'I didn't ask. Is it important?'

'I don't know. Are you alone now? Are you quite happy?'

'*Happy*?'

'You wouldn't like me to come along—'

'No. But thank you for suggesting it. After I've made those phone calls I shall turn in. It's been a tiring day.'

Miss Pink replaced the receiver with a strong feeling of anti-climax. She felt the constraint of her four walls and yet, if the visit had gone off so smoothly, with Campbell agreeing to see a doctor, it would be tempting fate to go outside for a breath of fresh air and risk an encounter with him. She compromised and went upstairs to stand in her dark bedroom at the side of the open window.

The tide had turned, but it was still high; she could hear the water rippling. From the hotel came the faint beat of a juke-box. A dog barked out on the lighthouse road, an owl called in the North Wood to be answered by another from the direction of the islands. There was no moon and only a few stars were visible. The night was mild and still. Campbell's van stood behind her own, their roofs gleaming in the light of the street lamp. There was no sign of the man. She was glad Beatrice had telephoned; without that brief conversation she would not have known he was alive. She wished he would come and drive away and give her proof that he existed, but the van waited mutely and nothing moved.

Chapter 8

Dan Butchart was the proprietor of the Isle Chrona, a large sweaty man who, out of season, did most of the work of the establishment. On Sunday mornings he drove to Morvern for the newspapers and, after the return of his white Volvo had been observed, a trickle of people made their way along the street, and the crofters came in from the lighthouse road. Collecting the Sunday paper was a ritual, on fine days an occasion for gossip.

This morning was dry if not exactly fine; there was an onshore breeze, and surf bloomed about the skerries. The islands looked near enough to touch. As people walked past Campbell's van they betrayed no interest in it; only on the quay, standing outside the hotel, did they look towards the vehicle – perhaps feeling that speculation was safe at a distance.

Miss Pink, coming down the steps of the hotel with her *Observer*, noting the sudden silence of a group of crofters about Duncan Millar, wondered what they had been saying, and forgot them as Beatrice approached wearing an ancient Burberry and gumboots. She looked as if she hadn't slept. She nodded and glanced meaningly at the crofters.

'I'll wait and walk back with you,' Miss Pink said, and went to stand at the edge of the quay. A few boats lay stranded by the ebb tide, but there was no sign of *Blue Zulu*. From this point the house that had been broken into, Camas Beag, was obvious at the head of a small clearing. She was still staring at it when Beatrice said from behind her, 'Did you hear him at his van last night?'

She turned. 'You think he couldn't start the engine? I didn't hear anyone at all. He must have changed his mind.'

They started to walk back to the street, Beatrice staring fixedly at Campbell's van.

'He went back to the island,' Miss Pink said comfortably.

'That's where he'll be now, having a lie-in. Do you realise that he's rowing? There was no outboard motor running last night.'

'People would hear the outboard.'

Miss Pink glanced sideways, made to comment, then changed her mind. 'But he's promised to come in for treatment?'

Beatrice threw her a wild look. 'Oh, yes. Monday. I promised to arrange it – the doctor's appointment. Monday morning.'

As Miss Pink was considering this, Esme overtook them, carrying a plastic bag like a baby in her arms, a posture sometimes adopted when one is carrying something heavy and breakable – like a bottle. Esme was tight-lipped and there was a defiant gleam in her eye. Tension did not become her; the plain features were sullen and when she spoke she sounded rude. 'You look ghastly,' she told Beatrice. 'Don't let it get you down.'

'*What*?'

'Only a manner of speaking. You're snappy this morning.'

'Don't be impertinent.'

Esme gaped. Miss Pink was blinking in surprise.

'I'm sorry,' Beatrice muttered. 'I didn't sleep much last night, and then . . . looking for Campbell, not knowing where he was, what he'd done, his state of mind – you know?'

'I should have been searching.' Esme was contrite.

'It's immaterial,' Miss Pink said. 'He's safe.'

'He was,' Beatrice put in and they stared at her, then at the van.

'You're keeping something back,' Miss Pink said, and her eyes went to Esme, who flared up like a firework.

'What makes you think that?'

'I meant Beatrice was keeping something back.'

'You looked at me!'

'All right, what are *you* keeping back?'

Esme's jaw dropped. Beatrice said quickly, 'I'm afraid we're back where we started. I told you what he said last night. I think he may have changed his mind after he left my house.'

'What makes you say that?' Miss Pink was at a loss, feeling that things were happening fast and yet she had little or no idea of what *was* happening. 'Just because he didn't move his van?

86

Where did he intend taking it?' Esme was following this with interest, making no move to interrupt.

Beatrice said, 'He wasn't going back to the island, except to collect his gear. It wasn't safe. He was adamant on that point: a quick visit to the island, back to the village and then he'd move the van. He said he'd sleep in it.'

'You might have told me that last night,' Miss Pink grumbled.

'I promised to keep it quiet. He was terrified of discovery; that was why he wouldn't sleep on the island: because we found his camp.'

'He's scared of *us*?'

'Coline would tell too many people.'

'Including the obvious one,' Esme said coldly. 'He had good cause to be terrified.'

Miss Pink rounded on her. '*Had*?'

'That's what I said.'

'The past tense?'

'Figure of speech.'

'So who did he have cause to be frightened of?'

'The same person who's sending anonymous letters.'

Before Miss Pink could respond to this, Beatrice said firmly, 'I want to go out to the island. Esme, will you take me in Sinclair's dinghy?'

'I'll come too,' Miss Pink said.

Beatrice hesitated, then nodded. 'All right. You could be an asset.' She seemed oblivious of her own rudeness.

The barnacle geese had gone when they approached the island and there was no sign of a boat. They landed and approached the camp-site in the birches. The tent was still there, flysheet and inner tent unfastened, the flaps hanging loose. 'Campbell?' Beatrice called, as Miss Pink had done yesterday. There was no reply. She looked at Miss Pink who swallowed, stepped forward and lifted a flap. No one was inside.

A meal had been prepared. The stove stood to one side, a can had been emptied, beans were in a dixie with a spoon. The dixie stood on the grass under the flysheet. Miss Pink touched the metal; it was cold.

'But it was too hot for the groundsheet,' she observed. 'He'd turned out the stove and taken the dixie off the burner. Just as he was about to start eating, he put down the dixie and came out. Why?'

They stood up and looked around. There was only a screen of birches behind the tent, which had been pitched close to the edge of the island where the ground dropped vertically for some thirty feet to the water. The heather was so dense that, suspecting an overhang, they didn't approach the edge. A few yards away an outcrop of sandstone formed a small prow. From this they could look down into water so clear that they could see the bottom ten feet below the surface.

'What do you think happened?' Esme asked.

Beatrice looked as if she were in shock. Miss Pink said, 'Well, he was disturbed at his supper, that's obvious.' She thought about this, then added, 'Not breakfast, I would think. . . . His sleeping bag is rolled up; one would imagine it would be unrolled if he'd just got out of it to make breakfast.'

'He wouldn't spend the night here,' Beatrice insisted. 'Whatever happened was important enough to make him leave everything and not come back.'

'You mean he jumped in his boat and pushed off?' Esme asked. 'So where did he go?'

'Where was he all day yesterday?' Miss Pink asked of Beatrice.

'He was on the mainland. He rowed to the shore when he saw us coming out to the islands and he hid among the rocks until we'd gone.'

'Then we'll go and see if he's there now.'

Esme took the boat by the shortest route to the shore and they came to a rock-fringed cove with a burn splashing down slabs at the back. The sand was covered with sheep droppings and was too deep and dry to hold footprints, but there was a corner which was probably awash at low tide and where a boat would be concealed from the view of anyone on the islands. Then they discovered a narrow sheep path running parallel with the shore, and where it crossed the burn there were the marks of cleated soles in the mud.

Miss Pink turned to Beatrice and said bluntly, 'He's gone, his boat's gone, but his van's still here. Do we start to look for him all over again, or is it a waste of time?'

Esme stared at her, then transferred her gaze to Beatrice who bit her lip and turned to look at the islands. 'I don't know where he is,' she said.

'Do you suggest we start looking?'

Beatrice didn't answer. 'We go back then?' Miss Pink pressed, 'and inform the police?'

Her tone roused the old lady from a kind of torpor. 'I'm sorry,' she said, 'but I can't help you. I'm at a loss. Yes, go back. The more people who know, the better – I suppose. We need a lot of people to search.' She held Miss Pink's eye. 'The last thing he told me,' she said, gathering strength, 'was that in no circumstances would he sleep on the island – because of these people who were after him. He would fetch his gear and drive out of the village to somewhere safe. I suggested that he should go to Debbie in Pitlochry; there was nothing to keep him here. The appointment with the doctor was a red herring – to convince people he wasn't going to run when in fact he meant to get as far away as possible. Obviously he hasn't gone.'

On their return, Beatrice directed Esme to bring the boat in to the steps below the hotel where it would be more accessible if it were needed later. The steps did not dry out at low tide. They left Esme at her cottage and went on to the police house. Joan Knox came to the door; her husband was at his dinner, she said, flustered. She showed them into an over-furnished sitting room and shortly afterwards Knox entered, apologising for keeping them waiting. Beatrice told him what they had found on the island.

He looked from one to the other. 'You reckon he's put an end to himself?' he asked, without surprise. He would have discussed the possibility with Ranald yesterday.

Beatrice said unhappily, 'I think he's finally lost control. He was close to the edge last night.'

Knox sighed. 'And there's no sign of his boat. It looks as if he went down the loch. I hope he didn't get as far as the open sea. Would he be that mad? A helicopter is what we're needing, but they'll say at headquarters the expense isn't warranted – they'll talk about the taxpayer. They know Campbell, you see. No one takes any notice of him now, but years ago someone took him seriously, so there is a record. And as mad as he is, he could have put ashore anywhere between here and the skerries, and if it was on the north side he might be holed up in an empty cottage like we thought yesterday. Are you suggesting we should search the same places all over again?'

'If he's mad, we should look for him,' Beatrice persisted. 'You'd look for a mental patient. What about bringing in dogs?'

'We wouldn't know where to start.'

Miss Pink said, 'If a tent were found in the mountains, abandoned in this fashion, a rescue team would be called in. It's good practice for them. No expense to the taxpayer, and they have dogs.'

Knox looked at her with admiration. 'Now that's a very good point, ma'am. I'll get in touch with the local team. Most of them come from around Morvern.'

But Sunday afternoon was not a good time to assemble a mountain rescue team; by two o'clock only six members had reached Sgoradale, and they had no dogs. Meanwhile a total of four boats had been put in the water, and throughout the remaining hours of daylight searchers scoured the loch shores looking, not for Campbell so much as for his boat which would be conspicuous. Like most Highlanders, Campbell wore drab clothing that would blend with heather and rock.

On the land Coline alerted her tenants and, by delegating much of the work, she saw to it that all the empty cottages – including Camas Beag – were searched a second time. On foot, on horseback and by Land Rover, every bothy and ruin was visited, and several crofters combed the North Wood with their sheepdogs. The situation took on an added urgency as the afternoon wore on and the wind freshened from the south-west.

'Front coming in,' Coline observed to Miss Pink as they came out of Lone Bothy. This had been a shepherd's cottage, but no one had lived in it for over a decade. Five miles inland from Sgoradale, in the lee of a mountain called Ben Tee, it was visited only by stalkers in bad weather, and by mountaineers using it as a way station or a base for exploring the central massif. It was unlocked, but too far from a road to attract vandals. There was nothing inside except bare boards and a grate, the ashes of which were cold. No one had stayed here recently.

Something moved on the slope of the mountain and Miss Pink's eyes sharpened, but before she could raise the binoculars Coline said, 'The deer are moving down. We're in for a wet night. I'm glad we don't have to walk back.'

Two ponies were tied to a rowan tree. A stocky cob had been found for Miss Pink, for which she'd been thankful as they'd splashed along the line of a rough track which was wet even after weeks of drought.

'He'd never come here anyway,' Coline remarked as they mounted and turned for home. 'There are too many places available to him around the village.'

'Everywhere has to be checked,' Miss Pink said. 'Even the improbable places. One doesn't know how his mind is working.'

'What made him flip, d'you suppose? After all, he's been here for ten years and stayed roughly at the same level: some lows and highs perhaps, but nothing ever approaching this kind of behaviour. Suddenly he goes to pieces. Do you have a theory?'

'I've only been here eight days!'

'That's a cop-out. You've listened to us, you know the background.'

'I wasn't investigating a crime. There was no need to ask probing questions. Remember, nothing happened out of the ordinary until Thursday night with the first fire, the abortive one. I've had no time to form an opinion.'

'You're hedging.'

'I assure you, I'm as bewildered as anyone else. I can't think why he should have chosen this moment to vanish . . . There's a spot of rain; what do you say to a turn of speed?'

Her pony leapt forward and Coline's followed. By the time the riders had slowed them to a hand gallop, awkward questions had been forgotten, to Miss Pink's relief. And as they came trotting along the rim of the escarpment all thoughts of

Campbell faded before the outlook. Only a few miles distant long skirts of rain were trailing up the loch.

The ponies jolted down the zig-zags and the first shower met them as they entered the stable yard.

Chapter 9

Sgoradale awoke to drizzle and low cloud, and to a feeling of disorientation as people remembered that one of their number was still missing. News had gone round that Debbie had been contacted, but her reactions weren't known. Her mother's home was not on the telephone and all that Knox could say was that Debbie had been seen by Pitlochry police and that Campbell was not with her.

As she lay in bed listening to water dripping from a faulty gutter, Miss Pink reflected that her own mood of indecision and vague resentment could prevail throughout the village. She thought she might stroll along to Feartag for coffee, although she would wait until later before calling Beatrice. They had spoken on the phone last evening after the visit to Lone Bothy, but there was nothing definite to say and they both recognised that speculation was futile. They had rung off with the ritual if forlorn hope that Campbell would turn up tomorrow.

She bathed and dressed and went next door for a bottle of milk. To her surprise Alec was behind the counter, not serving, but contemplating packets of cereal. She smiled in genuine pleasure and said the first thing that came to mind: 'How nice to see you about again,' then checked, thinking it might be unwise to refer to his condition, however obliquely.

But Alec was in no way disconcerted; in fact he returned her smile. 'I been about,' he said. 'It's just that I didn't go out till yesterday, and you were away with Lady Coline to Lone.'

After a fractional pause she said, 'You were looking for Ivar too?'

'He was.' Rose came in and bustled along the back of the counter. She glanced at two packets in Alec's hands, and said indulgently, 'Take them both, son, and go and get your breakfast.' She pushed him towards the living quarters and turned to Miss Pink, smiling brightly. 'Oh, yes, he was out searching for Ivar—' She grimaced and gestured at Alec's back. 'All pulling our weight, aren't we?' she went on loudly. 'Milk, was it, Miss Pink? Anything else?' She leaned over the counter, her face resuming its natural lines, her voice low. 'I let him out with his father for a wee while. They didn't go out of my sight: walked down the quay a ways, Alec with his dad's field-glasses. Gave him a breath of air, didn't it? Half an hour, I thought, that can't do any harm; half an hour a day, could it now?'

'Perhaps increasing it each day?' Miss Pink suggested. 'Or going out more than once?'

'Well . . . ' Rose considered, fingering her lips, eyeing Miss Pink uncertainly, 'the outing yesterday didn't seem to take too much out of him; maybe he can do a little more today, with me or his father. There's no question of allowing him out on his own. I mean—' she caught herself suddenly '—he could do himself an injury: fall off the quay, walk in front of a car. There's no knowing what might happen, is there?'

Miss Pink went home, reflecting that she was only a visitor; it wasn't her place to suggest that protection could go too far. She was eating her breakfast when Alec shuffled jerkily past her window, alone but talking with great animation. Unable to help herself she opened the door and stared after him – and her expression softened. His irregular progress was occasioned by a small round sheepdog puppy which was alternately scampering at his heels and sitting down to worry its scarlet leash. She turned, smiling, to find herself observed by Rose who was standing in her own doorway.

'A good idea,' Miss Pink said. 'I'm surprised he's accepted a substitute so quickly – but delighted.'

Rose ignored the gist of this and said quickly, as if she'd been waiting for the chance, 'Maybe we do protect him too much. I thought I'd take a chance and let him out on his own. He's not to go near the edge of the quay, mind. He'll not be out of the sight of one of us at any time.'

Miss Pink returned to her breakfast and the problem of what she should do on a poor day in a Highland village when one of its residents was missing. She found the inability to reach a decision annoying and something of a bore, but this was to be her last experience of *ennuie* for some considerable time and it was short-lived.

The interruption came when she was drinking her second cup of coffee. She was reading a book review in yesterday's *Observer* when she caught the sound of someone running fast along the road – a woman in high heels. She heard the bell ring on the Post Office door and raised voices, muted as the door swung shut. She sat unmoving, her coffee forgotten. She could still hear a voice, even through the party wall. It moderated a little, there were moments when it ceased altogether; finally she heard the bell again and then, to her amazement, the clack of heels terminated with the banging of a fist on her own door. She opened it to Joan Knox, her hair awry and her eyes anguished.

'Have you seen my boy, miss? Hamish – did you see him this morning?'

'Why, no.' Miss Pink stood back. 'Won't you come in?'

'No. I got to find him. I can't go to *her* . . . ' She gestured savagely at the nurse's house.

The police car came out of the Knoxes' drive and roared along the street in low gear. It stopped and Knox got out and came quickly to Miss Pink's door. He took his wife's arm. She shook him off. 'The boy's gone,' he told Miss Pink, putting an arm round Joan's shoulders. She whirled and punched him in the mouth. They fell apart, Knox holding his jaw, Joan cringing. As the woman opened her mouth for what might well be a shriek, Miss Pink pushed her firmly indoors and into a chair where she collapsed in a paroxysm of sobbing.

'Shut the door, Mr Knox,' Miss Pink said. 'Then put the kettle on and pour some brandy. You'll find everything in that corner cupboard. Take a dram yourself.'

She sat opposite Joan, alert for any renewal of hostilities, but the woman had lost all initiative. Knox busied himself as directed and eventually, with the aid of tissues, the brandy and Miss Pink's stern supervision, she regained control of herself although still shaken by the occasional racking sob. At last, and without a word being said, she looked at Knox with eyes that were still hostile but which seemed to hold a plea. There was fear too; she was terrified, but not – Miss Pink thought – of her husband.

95

Knox took it upon himself to explain, shifting uneasily under that intent stare. 'There was a bundle of clothes, a dummy like, in his bed this morning. She went up when he didn't come down to breakfast. His clothes are gone – he's been out all night.'

'He's sixteen.' Miss Pink was equable. 'I've no doubt he has friends among other lads: virtually young men. It's not unheard-of for an adolescent boy to stay out all night. It's very thoughtless, but young people aren't always thoughtful.'

'It's unnatural,' Joan said. 'He never did this before; he's been set a bad example.'

Knox opened his mouth and closed it again.

Miss Pink said, 'You don't know how many times he's done it and come back without your knowing he ever left his room.'

'Then what's keeping him?'

Miss Pink looked at Knox, who said wildly, 'He stole a car and ran out of petrol, or he's with his mates in Morvern. Or someone got drunk and couldn't drive him home. *He* got drunk. Christ! (beg pardon, ma'am) anything could have happened.'

'That Millar were out yesterday.' Joan made it sound like an accusation.

'Hamish could run rings round him.'

'He's mad. He'd kill Hamish.' She stopped, her hand over her mouth.

'Alec was with his father yesterday,' Miss Pink said firmly. 'They'd never let him out on his own.'

'How do you know?' The hostility was turned on Miss Pink. 'Our boy got out, didn't he? Maybe that Alec Millar was out all night. Maybe they met.' As she envisaged the confrontation, her mouth widened.

'No!' Miss Pink said, so loudly that the rising hysteria was quenched. She went on, enunciating very clearly. 'Rose Millar is so concerned about her son that I doubt if she goes to sleep. A mouse couldn't move in that house at night without her hearing it.'

'He's a powerful man,' Joan said. 'He could get past his mother.'

'And his father?'

'Duncan Millar would egg him on. They always hated us – poachers and thieves, the lot of 'em.'

'That's enough!' Knox flushed dangerously. 'You'll have to make allowances, ma'am,' he said, dropping his voice a fraction. 'She's hysterical; I'll get the doctor to her—'

'Not the doctor, nor yet that nurse, so-called. I'm all right. I'm frightened, that's all. I want to know where my boy is.'

Miss Pink said, 'We can't do anything about finding him until you calm down. At the moment you're claiming all the attention for yourself. If you go home with Mr Knox quietly and have Mary MacLeod in for company, the rest of us will start looking for Hamish.'

'Where will you look?'

'We shall make enquiries methodically; we know the drill—' Miss Pink stopped, appalled, and Joan responded as if cued.

'There are two people missing now.'

There was a grim triumph in the statement, as if she felt herself vindicated.

Anne Wallace received her visitor without surprise. 'Yes, I know he's missing,' she said calmly. 'Come in, please.' She ushered Miss Pink into her sitting room. 'What can I do?' she asked. They both remained standing.

'Some effort has to be made to find out where Hamish is,' Miss Pink said. 'Some compromise between reporting him as a missing person and ignoring his absence completely.'

'So what do you suggest?'

Miss Pink felt at a disadvantage and this annoyed her. 'Aren't you bothered?' she asked.

Anne nodded as if she'd been expecting that question. 'I'm not concerned,' she admitted. 'I'm interested as a neighbour, but not professionally. If I was to get involved every time a teenager stays out all night, I'd have ulcers inside a month.'

'I see your point. May I ask how you knew about Hamish?'

'Mr Knox phoned me. He was bothered about his wife. She was hysterical when she found the boy's bed hadn't been slept in; Knox panicked and asked me to bring a sedative.'

'Did you?'

97

'Oh, no. I made him see reason and told him to talk some sense into his wife. So how did you get involved? I'm sorry, that sounds rude.'

'Not at all.' Miss Pink told her about the Knoxes' visit.

'And are you really going to look for Hamish?' Anne asked.

'Knox is ringing the hospitals in Morvern and Inverness. He's contacting his friends in the police without reporting it officially. Since Joan Knox's outburst the affair can't be kept secret, so while he's making his enquiries I intend to ask people if they have any information that might help. It's the least I can do. If all the results prove negative, I expect Knox will make an official report. Ultimately it's up to him, and he's under pressure from the boy's mother.'

'No doubt.' The tone was dry.

'She's hostile to you,' Miss Pink said bluntly. The woman stared at her. 'Is it a coincidence,' Miss Pink asked, 'that she should be hostile at this moment, or does she make a connection?'

'A . . . connection between – what?' The woman was white. Her eyes narrowed and she fidgeted, but professional calm had not deserted her. 'It's not a coincidence,' she said at length. 'Hamish is spoiled, and only the fact that his father manages to assert some authority keeps the boy straight – and not quite, at that. He's got a nasty line in practical jokes. He played a trick on me last summer which was quite outrageous and I shan't forget it in a hurry. Of course, Joan Knox won't wear it; Hamish is a *good* boy.' It was a spurt of venom that was gone in an instant. 'Joan and I are not on visiting terms,' she concluded coldly.

'So,' Miss Pink said with a burst of joviality that clearly startled the nurse, 'I'll complete my interrogation with the traditional question: When did you last see Hamish?'

Anne seemed undecided as to whether her visitor were mad and harmless, or devious. She answered carefully, 'I didn't see him yesterday. I don't have many calls to make at a weekend: it's a morning round only on a Sunday. In the afternoon I stayed indoors and I wouldn't see anyone pass the gateway unless I was looking out at that moment. My hedge is pretty high, as you

98

see; it hides the street from this window. I did see him Saturday afternoon. I was coming home from Morvern and he was turning in to the lodge drive. He was on a pony. That would be some time after five, around five-thirty.'

'And what do you think has happened to him?'

Anne smiled. 'There are no witnesses to this conversation, so I'd say that either he got into trouble along with the local lads or he's played a trick that's rebounded on him.'

'Who are his friends?'

'You'll have to ask his father.'

'And Campbell? When did you see him last?'

'At the fire – no, he wasn't there. Friday morning probably; he was out in his boat.'

'Have you any theories about his disappearance?'

'I assume that he put out to sea and just kept going until his fuel ran out.'

'You mean suicide? Why should he kill himself?'

'I think he went mad – burning his home down like that.'

'She's wary.' Miss Pink leaned back in her chair and sighed. 'The nurse is wary, Knox is angry, his wife is terrified. And I'm at a loss. What about you? What's your reaction to this latest development?'

'Too much is happening; I'm bewildered.' Beatrice suited actions to words, absently moving the coffee things about the table in her sitting room.

'I came straight here from Anne's house,' Miss Pink said. 'I couldn't face anyone else for the moment. I needed to talk to someone – not to put too fine a point on it – someone like myself.'

'You flatter me.'

'You know what I mean.'

'Of course. Well, what's to do now?'

'I'm hoping that shortly Knox will have to do something himself.'

'He can't expect you to do anything.'

'It's a peculiar situation. He doesn't want to bring the authorities in officially in case the boy is playing some kind of trick. It's obvious that he knows Hamish does indulge in practical jokes. Anne is in no doubt about it. On the other hand, the boy could have met with an accident. But then there's Campbell's disappearance; can there be a connection? If Hamish *is* up to mischief, he's placed his father in an awful dilemma. He needs all the help he can get.'

'Let's walk to the lodge and talk to Coline. By the time we get there either Knox will have news – or he must come to a decision. If his wife doesn't make him, Coline will as soon as she hears what you have to say.'

The rain had stopped and a stiff breeze was blowing up the loch driving the next shower before it, obscuring the skerries and veiling the sodden slopes. As they turned into the street Miss Pink said, 'I'm sure Rose Millar knew that Hamish was missing when I was in the shop at breakfast time, but she didn't mention it.'

'Wait! Can that be a whimbrel?'

They stopped and listened, their eyes on the birds feeding at the edge of the tide. 'Mostly curlew,' Beatrice murmured. 'Sorry, you were saying Rose knew Hamish was missing before you did?'

'She was too concerned to impress on me that Alec went out only once yesterday, and that with his father. But he was out alone this morning. So then she implied that today was the first time he was unaccompanied. None of that cuts any ice with Joan Knox, who says Alec could even have been out last night. If Hamish comes to grief, it's obvious who she'll hold responsible.'

'A foregone conclusion.' Beatrice turned away from the birds. 'They're all curlew. Oh dear, can this be more trouble?'

Esme Dunlop was bearing down on them. 'How are you?' she called. 'Lovely soft day – we need the rain. Seen anything?'

'Nothing,' Miss Pink said. 'But one keeps looking: for wreckage, clothing, anything. And you?'

'Hell! You think he's in the loch?' She swung round, taking in the woods and the escarpment. 'I hadn't got that far – wondering whether he was on land or in the sea. He's gone and that's it as far as I'm concerned. Good riddance.'

'You didn't like him,' Miss Pink observed lightly.

'You can say that again. If you ask me, he was behind all the mischief in this village from the word go: car thefts, the police car, the heavy breather, anonymous letters – particularly letters.'

'Campbell sent you that?'

'Who's talking about Campbell?'

'I was.'

'Oh.' There was a long silence, then she laughed. 'I was talking about Hamish.'

Miss Pink looked mildly interested. 'So you had phone calls in addition to the anonymous letter. May one ask what was said?'

'Nothing. It was a heavy breather – giggling too, but no words.'

'What time did he call?'

'After midnight.'

'You answered the phone.'

'Once. Why? Someone else was getting calls, or everybody? I see, you're not talking. Well, take my word for it; there won't be any more telephone calls.'

'He could start again, unless he's had a bad fright.'

'He won't be coming back.' It was said smugly but, as if the words had been too much for her own equilibrium, Esme's face fell. 'Or is that wishful thinking?' she asked.

'Gay as a puppy,' Beatrice remarked when they'd parted from Esme and were walking up the Lamentation Road.

'Jolly,' Miss Pink corrected absently. 'How I detest this corruption of the language. So she got heavy breather calls too. She was subdued, now she's back to normal – and Hamish is missing. How much does she know about his disappearance?'

'Nothing,' Beatrice said promptly. 'She's far too frank about her relief.'

'Have you never heard of double-bluff?'

Beatrice shrugged. 'She's wrong. The business with the police car could have involved Hamish conniving with local boys, but anonymous letters and phone calls and car thefts –

never. That wasn't him; he's just . . . well . . . naughty.'

At the lodge Coline had learned something of the village gossip, but by no means all. 'It's scarcely enough to have hysterics about,' she said, serving sherry: 'A sixteen-year-old not coming home at night.'

'Who told you?' Miss Pink asked.

'Rose Millar. Joan Knox didn't turn up for work – we employ her full-time now that Debbie's left – and I called the police house. I couldn't get through, so I rang the Post Office to ask if Joan were ill. I got a pretty cool reception there, I can tell you. Apparently Joan accused Rose of nameless horrors in respect of Hamish.'

'Alec, actually; she's accusing Alec,' Miss Pink said. 'You couldn't get through to Knox because he was calling the hospitals and various friends in the police. And Hamish was home during the evening; he left a dummy in his bed. So there was an intention to deceive his parents should they look in on him.'

'That's a different kettle of fish. Now why would he do that?'

'Do what?' Ranald entered in his stocking feet. 'Excuse me, ladies; we've been battening down the hatches, or rather I have. I miss Campbell. We'll have to get Sinclair and Millar to give us a hand, m'dear. First storms after a long drought always find all the weak places.'

'Melinda says Hamish was out all night and left a dummy in his bed.'

'Was he now! Why did he do that?'

'That's what we're wondering. He's missing.'

'What! Like Campbell? Why wasn't I told?'

'Sweetie, I've known since ten o'clock, but I didn't think it important.'

'Two people missing? It's dead serious. What's Knox doing about it?'

Miss Pink told him. Beatrice said, 'I wonder if Knox has thought to get in touch with Hamish's friends. There are a number of lads on the crofts along the lighthouse road.'

'I think we should find out.' Coline rose and left the room.

Ranald stared after her, then turned to Beatrice. 'What do you think? You know him.'

'Not well; I don't employ him. You'd have seen more of him.'

'True. He's a nice enough lad. Flora was a bit impatient with him. Of course, she can ride. She had to teach him. . . . Wonder what Knox has discovered.' He made to rise, remembered his manners and sank back in his chair.

'Was Hamish out yesterday when everyone else was searching for Campbell?' Miss Pink asked. 'After we returned from the islands and told you about the meal in the tent?'

'He was on the moor behind Fair Point, on horseback. I saw him once or twice. I went out to the light again in the Land Rover.'

'Did you see him when he brought the pony back?'

'No, there would be no need. He'd put the tack away and turn the pony out himself. He knows what to do.'

'I suppose all your ponies are accounted for?'

'What? You think he's gone off with a pony like Campbell took a boat? Impossible. The ponies are all there anyway – I gave them some hay this morning. I'm the dogsbody now.'

Coline returned, looking concerned. 'Knox has drawn a blank,' she said. 'He's mystified and unhappy. Joan's giving him no peace. He says Hamish had no close friends among the local lads, but he's spoken to several of the fathers; no one else is missing, and no other boy who's available at the moment can help. I told Knox he must report the business to the superintendent at Morvern and let him take it from there. Any other parent would do that; Knox has to stop thinking of appearances.'

'You're thinking of the police car in Anne's drive,' Beatrice said.

'Well, that, and worse.' Seeing Miss Pink's raised eyebrows, Coline added, 'One always wondered about the car thefts, you know.'

'That was Hell's Angels,' Ranald spluttered. 'I'd never have employed Hamish if I'd thought he was a thief.'

'You didn't,' Coline said. '*I* did. Why am I talking in the past tense? Hamish *is* employed by us, when he's here. That

103

reminds me: Flora will have to come home and look after those ponies. I haven't the time or the inclination to exercise them, and we'll have to start feeding soon. You shouldn't have given them hay today, sweetie; there's enough grass.' She clutched her temples. 'I'm getting distracted – and I should be working on a book! I'm going to call Flora; she won't like it, but she's got to think of her responsibilities. I don't hold with children persuading their parents to buy animals and then leaving Mum to do the chores when it suits – particularly when Mum is by way of being the breadwinner.' Venom had crept into her voice and Ranald shifted uncomfortably.

'What's the next step, once the authorities at Morvern have been informed?' Beatrice asked.

'If they think he's in this locality, they'll bring in a search party,' Miss Pink said, picking up her cue. 'But it's more likely that they'll look in amusement arcades and cafés – anywhere that youngsters hang out in Morvern and Inverness. You can't search meticulously unless there's some indication that the missing person is in that area, as we thought Campbell was.'

'I still think he's here,' Ranald said. 'Campbell, I mean. They'll find his boat or his body in the sea. It's obvious; he went mad and drowned himself.'

They stayed to lunch at the lodge and afterwards Beatrice walked home across the park while Miss Pink, pleading the need for exercise, strolled along the drive to the highway. A few yards down the Lamentation Road she came to a gate at the back of the terrace where Esme lived. Only the upper windows of the houses were visible, the lower ones hidden by walled yards. Along the field side of the wall a path, muddied by small hooves, looked as if it would run past the back of the hotel towards the shore of the loch.

It was a nasty slimy little path on a slope, but Miss Pink was in boots and she took her time. The slope was wooded and there were still enough leaves on the trees to obscure all but a grey glimmer of the hotel and its outbuildings as she traversed behind them. Her boots left clear prints in the mud, superimposed on sheep tracks. There were no other human prints, but before the rain came yesterday no one could have left prints except where the burn crossed the path.

She reached that place and found an appreciable increase in the volume of water coming down. Another heavy shower was approaching, heralded by a gusty wind that sent white horses running over the surface of the loch. Spray burst on the rocks and she wondered if Campbell's tent was still standing. Looking towards the islands, the furthest of which was now obscured, something caught her eye – something close to the mainland shore – but when she studied the heaving water the object had disappeared.

She scrambled down to the beach and found an overhanging corner where she could shelter from the shower. From here the point on the far side of the cove was in full view. Two oystercatchers were standing on the weed, facing into the wind, their shoulders hunched. There wasn't much wrong with her eyes; she could distinguish their scarlet bills and legs.

The tide was lower than she'd thought. Kelp bobbed up, branched at the top, and vanished below the next wave. She hadn't seen kelp since California, and then there'd been sea otters diving through it. She'd thought that this kind of weed was a Pacific species; surely Atlantic kelp was only exposed at the lowest tides, and this tide had two hours to go before the turn. Dry and sheltered in her rock corner, she stared out at the water and pondered her ignorance. After a while her gaze became fixed and she emerged to move along the beach. The oystercatchers took off with wild calls. She ignored them.

She walked into the water until she was wading. When the waves were slapping her thighs she climbed on to the rocks and, stumbling across the bladderweed, reached the point she had been aiming for: within twenty feet of the kelp that now, with the falling tide, was regularly revealed in each trough of the waves.

It was no kelp but a human arm.

Chapter 10

Sgoradale was suddenly a centre of activity, intensifying from the moment when Knox saw the thing in the water. Miss Pink had stressed that it had been immersed for a while and, when they drew near, coming in by sea, she was glad that she'd taken that precaution. The water was lower now and, in the heaving sea, a more or less globular object appeared at the end of the arm, all colour washed out: dark hair plastered to a splintered skull. The arm was no longer projecting but floating limply on the surface.

They went back to the village, Knox informed his superiors at Morvern and was told to guard the cove. Miss Pink told him to take a gun. 'For the birds,' she said, when he looked puzzled. He raised no objection when she accompanied him to the boat.

The weather was worsening and the sea rising but, once in the lee of the islands, they were sheltered from the wind. They landed in the cove. Gulls were swooping at the head and he fired at them wildly – a useless gesture. From cracked white bone, empty sockets regarded the shore, the head swaying on the stalk of a neck. The damage had been done already by crabs; gulls could do little more.

'It's been there days,' he said.

She calculated. 'A day and a half. Miss Swan saw him on Saturday night.'

'He must have tied something round himself and jumped in.'

Questions crowded her mind but they were technical; she was appalled at the questions that he must be asking himself, had been ever since she told him of her grisly discovery. For him the body itself could have little importance compared with Hamish's present whereabouts.

Their enforced intimacy did not last long. The shoulders of that dreadful form had just appeared when a boat emerged from the islands with four people aboard. 'It's the Chief

Inspector,' Knox said, and walked down to the water.

The men came ashore and pulled the boat up. The boatman was old Sinclair. He studied the partially exposed body without surprise; he wouldn't be unfamiliar with the appearance of a body recovered from the sea. Knox introduced Miss Pink and she found herself scrutinised by pale blue eyes in a pale face. Detective Chief Inspector Pagan belied his name: short ginger hair under a flat cap, a smart trench-coat and dark tie implied conformity. His sergeant had the blunt features, the alert bearing of a bright Gorbals youth, but he wasn't a youth, and the creases in his tanned cheeks spoke of the kind of wasting that goes with hard training. His name was Steer and he moved like a boxer. Pagan regarded the body without expression, but Steer had the look of a boy presented with his first bicycle. The fourth man was the diver.

There was no need to use a boat. The diver approached the body from the rocks and seemed scarcely out of his depth when his head submerged, giving the impression of a monster nosing its prey. He was gone only a short time before returning to the rocks and the other officers. From the beach Miss Pink and Sinclair watched in silence.

After a short exchange the diver went back to the body, submerged a second time and suddenly the torso gave a little jump before keeling over on the surface. The diver's head appeared, then the rest of him as he waded shoreward dragging the corpse. He pulled it from the water and it lay on the wet sand, rope trailing behind it. The rope was tied round the ankles.

The body lay on its face. Steer turned it over. Pagan looked towards Miss Pink, who approached. Sinclair followed her. 'Does anyone recognise the clothes?' Pagan asked.

'Campbell was wearing a tartan shirt the last time that I saw him,' she said. 'That shirt is a check material. Apart from that I couldn't say who this is – no one could except his dentist.'

Pagan nodded. 'Someone hated this man badly. It wasn't enough to batter his skull in, they had to tie him to the boat's painter and sink the boat – although he'd have been dead by then, of course.'

'How was the boat sunk?' Miss Pink asked.

Pagan's eyes were bright as a stalking cat's; he only looked like a bureaucrat. 'How?' he repeated. 'The diver reckons the plug isn't in the boat, but what is in it, is some big rocks. This chap' – he motioned to the body – 'was tied to a rock as well as being fastened to the boat.'

The diver had returned to the water and must have cleared the rocks because suddenly the boat surfaced, upside down. He pulled it to the shore with some difficulty. The name *Blue Zulu* was on the prow, and the plug was missing.

'Like I said,' Pagan observed, 'he meant business. Didn't study his tides though; didn't realise this gentleman was going to expose himself at low water, did he?'

'This was a man two days ago,' old Sinclair said. 'The corp is still entitled to respect.'

'Ah, yes.' Pagan seemed to glow. 'You liked the man, did you?'

Miss Pink looked at Sinclair and saw an old man demonstrating disapproval. She looked at Knox and saw, behind the cold policeman's eyes . . . terror.

While Steer produced a camera and started taking pictures, Pagan drew Miss Pink aside. 'I understand you also discovered Campbell's tent,' he said. 'I'd like you to show it to me.'

'Certainly. And you ought to know that yesterday, before the rain, there was at least one boot mark by the burn here.'

'Show me.'

They scrambled to the path and he stared at cleated prints in the mud. 'Those are mine,' she said. 'No one else had made any tracks since the rain. The track I saw yesterday could have been Campbell's; he's wearing boots.'

'When was he seen last?'

'To my knowledge, on Saturday evening.'

'Yes, the boatman said he visited Miss Swan. Do you know why?'

She told him about the message Beatrice had left in the tent. 'He came at her instigation. Miss Swan thought he should have professional help. We were all afraid of what he might do to himself; we thought him paranoid. He said he would come ashore, take his van and drive somewhere safe.'

'And his van is still in the village.' He held her eye. 'I've heard about you, ma'am; you're friendly with Professor Brodie. You remember – the pathologist? He did the autopsies when the girls were killed on the Isle of Skye.'*

'That was ten years ago. Is he still going strong?'

'Like a spring chicken. So I know of you and I'd welcome your help. These remote communities close up when the CID arrives.'

Their eyes locked. 'What do you want to know?' she asked.

'It's a curious thing. Less than two hours after a lad's reported missing from this village, a man is found murdered.'

'It sounds odd, but while the body was in the sea – assuming it's Campbell's – young Hamish was helping to search for him. And my finding the body was accidental; no one else has cause to visit the cove.'

'Except people coming to take another look at the man's camp-site. Show me that tent. One thing,' he added archly as they walked to the boat, 'a whole village may be under suspicion, but I do have one objective witness.'

She returned his smile, wondering how much faith he put in her cooperation.

The body was placed in Sinclair's boat and, accompanied by Steer and the diver, conveyed to the village. Pagan had relieved Steer of the camera and Knox ferried his superior and Miss Pink to the island where Campbell had pitched his tent. The geese had disappeared from the bay, which was now an inhospitable place: colourless and swept by rain.

Sheltered by the scrub birch the tent was still standing, apparently untouched since she had closed it yesterday on leaving. Knox was told to stand beside it to show the scale while Pagan took photographs. The constable's face was wooden. The flysheet was unzipped to reveal the spoon in the pan of beans, then Pagan opened the inner tent. The interior looked undisturbed: the stove, the sleeping bag, the remaining dixies, cup and cutlery, the empty can and the full ones. Knox and Miss Pink held the flaps aside so that there should be enough light for photographs. Pagan put everything in plastic bags, then they

* *Over the Sea to Death.*

109

struck the tent and carried the loads down to the boat.

On their return to the village Pagan had them identify the different houses – what could be seen of them through the rain – eliciting everything they could tell him about the inhabitants. He was double-checking. As Knox responded to the seemingly casual questions the Inspector's pale eyes noted Miss Pink's reactions. They were halfway home when Knox eased up on the throttle and asked, 'Is anything being done about my boy?'

'I'm sorry about that,' Pagan said. 'They're looking in all the likely places. That's not a CID matter, of course. Maybe there'll be some news when we get back.'

'Is there a connection?' It burst out of him as if he couldn't arrest it.

'You know better than to ask me a question like that.' Pagan was almost avuncular. 'I expect your lad's in the big city spending his money on fruit machines and fags. He'll be back when he gets cold and hungry and he's got nowhere to sleep, mark my words.'

No one answered him. They looked at the approaching shore and a further question hung in the air: if not in the big city, where?

Miss Pink changed into dry clothes and walked to Feartag. Getting no response to her knock, she went round the house and came on Beatrice filling a basket with peats from the stack under the gable end. 'You must have had a wet walk,' the old lady said pleasantly, picking up the basket.

Miss Pink was dumbfounded for a moment before lurching forward. 'Here, let me give you a hand.'

'No, it's light. You shut the gate. You can bring the logs in and close the cellar door, if you don't mind. The wind's getting up; we're in for a wet night.'

Miss Pink obeyed in a kind of stupor, unable to credit that the grapevine had broken down. She closed the gate, mounted a couple of steps to the terrace, closed the cellar door, picked up a basket of logs and followed her hostess into the sitting room. She said firmly, 'I would suggest a good stiff drink.'

Beatrice stared at her. 'Something's happened.' She moved

to the sideboard, then stopped. 'You may as well tell me. I'm prepared now.'

'I doubt that. Campbell met with an accident.'

'Dear God! I can guess what you mean. So he did commit suicide?'

'He's dead.'

'Poor fellow. And yet he gave me no indication at all. You amaze me. Could I have stopped it? I could have influenced him, I'm sure, if I'd known how his mind was working. I was very obtuse. Could—'

'He didn't commit suicide. He—'

'You mean he really did have an accident. His boat capsized? Or did—'

'Beatrice, let me tell you. He was murdered.'

'No.' It was quiet, little more than an exhalation. Miss Pink outlined the salient points: the fractured skull, the weights, the plug removed from *Blue Zulu*.

'I always loved that name,' Beatrice said. 'But the name can be used again, can't it, even though the boat's gone?'

Miss Pink stood up and went to the sideboard. Beatrice sat down and allowed herself to be waited on. She drank a glass of brandy as if it were milk while Miss Pink gave the less horrible details of her visits to the cove with Pagan, Steer and Knox, 'who sound like a musical hall turn,' she concluded.

'How can you talk like that?'

'Defence mechanism. I don't find Pagan amusing – and he's definitely bad news for the murderer.'

'He's intelligent?'

'He and his sergeant. They're a good team. Most investigative teams are; the best men gravitate to each other. I daresay he'll be here as soon as he's finished at Campbell's old cottage. He's gone up there with the others. He'll need to talk to you because you were the last innocent person to see Campbell.'

'The last innocent . . . ? Of course, someone else had to see him. There's nothing I can tell the police other than what I've told you.' She sat up suddenly, spilling her drink. 'But this is appalling! Is it – can it be someone in the village? No, that's ridiculous. But then – was Campbell right all the time? It *was* some form of secret service activity?'

Miss Pink sipped her sherry thoughtfully. 'I hadn't even considered it,' she confessed. 'What I've been occupied with ever since I found the body, and what concerns Knox to the exclusion of anything else, is the disappearance of Hamish.'

'What's that got to do with Campbell?'

'No one knows, although several people may be speculating. Knox looks as if he dreads the worst. Joan will maintain that there's no connection at all.'

'And she'd be right. If Hamish had anything to do with Campbell's death, he wouldn't have waited a whole day before running away. And he has no reason to . . . oh, this is stupid; no one had a reason for killing Campbell, no one in the village anyway.'

Miss Pink was staring at a water-colour of an iceberg. 'Someone had a reason,' she murmured, 'and if you do exclude espionage, only local people are left. The motive isn't all that elusive either. Greed and sex are out: Campbell seems to have had nothing valuable and he surely wasn't a philanderer. But he was a snooper. The motive was probably elimination; he got in someone's way, or he learned something – something connected with crime?'

'Not in Sgoradale. We don't have crime.'

'Hamish's disappearance?'

'You don't think—'

'No, he disappeared after Campbell was killed.'

'There was a knock at the front door. 'That will be the police,' Miss Pink said. 'Do you want me to stay?'

'That's kind of you, but I can cope. Why don't you stroll through the North Wood and come back later?'

'It's nearly dark. I'm going home. Ring me when they've gone.'

She followed Beatrice to the front door. Two strange men were on the step, one with a photographer's bag. The other one said brightly, 'You're Miss Swan? We're from the *Northern Mail*. May we come in?'

'How can we help you?' Beatrice made no move to admit them. Miss Pink hovered in the rear.

'You were the last person to see Campbell alive.'

'I was?' Beatrice was startled. 'I'm sorry, I didn't catch your name.'

'Colin MacAllister. We were told—'

'The last person to see Mr Campbell alive was his mur derer.'

'Of course.' He looked past her to encounter Miss Pink's penetrating stare.

'You can get the facts from the police,' Beatrice said. 'Those that they're able to make public, that is. I'd think it would impede the investigation if they divulged everything they know. All I can tell you is that Mr Campbell was helping me on Friday afternoon, and he left here at five o'clock.'

'Why did he come here on Saturday night?'

The old eyes flashed. 'Is this normal practice?'

'Is what normal practice?'

Miss Pink moved forward. 'Mr MacAllister, you must be the first reporter Miss Swan has come into contact with, and you're not making a very good impression. She was quite right when she said you must go to the police for facts; as for a human story, we can tell you no more than that Campbell was a good worker. We knew nothing of his private life; that wasn't our business, and speculation is a waste of time and energy. And now we mustn't keep you any longer. Thank you for calling. Good night, gentlemen.'

Back in the sitting room Beatrice said, 'I've changed my mind. Please stay. The police I can handle, but not that kind of thing.'

Miss Pink shrugged. 'They were doing their job. . . . And the television people will be here tomorrow. It's a sensational story – and with Hamish missing as well, the Press are bound to speculate. I was tempting fate to use the word; they'll do nothing else.'

'What did you mean when you said earlier that Knox was thinking the worst?'

'Now that's an odd thing. Before Campbell's body was found I thought – given the premise that Hamish was the village joker – he could well have run into more trouble than a boy could

113

deal with. That was what I thought originally. Then I found Campbell's body.'

'That makes a difference?'

'It must do. Who killed Campbell? Is it possible that Hamish isn't a victim but a murderer?'

'You know how I felt about arson, so this leaves me unmoved. A sixteen-year-old boy!'

'There have been younger murderers.'

Beatrice shook her head and leaned back in her chair. 'This is all too much for me. Murder in Sgoradale! But we don't know anything, do we?'

'We don't know who killed Campbell.'

'That's horrible. It has to be someone local?' Beatrice was begging to be contradicted.

Miss Pink gave the question thought. 'It doesn't have to be,' she admitted. 'Someone could have left a car on a peat track out on the moor where it wouldn't be seen from the Lamentation Road, or he could have been dropped by an accomplice to hide in the woods and be picked up after he'd done what he came for. There were two visits to Campbell's cottage on Friday evening: the intruder who knocked him down, and the arsonist. Two visits but, we assume, one visitor. Of course, we only have Campbell's word for those incidents, and now there's no way of finding out how much of what he told us was truth and how much fantasy, if any. Was someone else similarly frustrated, and killed him to be on the safe side?'

The police came late, presumably after interviewing other people. Pagan looked tired and Steer had lost some of his alertness, but once they were seated and furnished with drinks Pagan got down to business, wanting to know what time Campbell had left Feartag on the Saturday evening, after the clandestine visit. About ten o'clock, Beatrice told him. Then he wanted to know everything Campbell had said, and this she found difficult to recall in view of his fantasies, which were inclined to make one nod if he got on to one of his hobby horses. 'Such as?' Pagan asked.

'People watching his house. Arsonists.'

'Yes, I want to come back to that. What did he say about his future movements, starting with when he left this house?'

'He said that in no circumstances would he sleep on the island, that he would go back and pick up his gear and drive to somewhere that was safe.'

'Where was his boat? Where did he come ashore?'

'I don't know. I assumed it was at the mouth of the river, below this house. It was high tide. . . . But I hadn't heard an outboard. . . . Of course, he was rowing; I'd forgotten that.'

Miss Pink said, 'I don't think he'd row all the way from the island. I've been thinking that he put ashore in the cove – the one where I found the body – and walked to the village. That would be safer if you didn't want to be seen. It's not easy to get out of the way if you're in a boat.'

'Out of the way of what, for example?'

'A bullet?'

'We don't know how he was killed. There may be a bullet wound under those fractures, but so far it looks like a blunt instrument.' His tone changed. 'So we have him starting back to his boat around ten o'clock. How would he go from here?'

'Along the street and the quay,' Beatrice said. 'He'd work up through the trees on the other side of the hotel to strike the path along the south shore – the little sheep trod.'

'There are lights as far as the end of the quay. How would he go if he didn't want to be seen?'

'Providing he had a torch, he could go up river for a short distance, then through the park and cross the Lamentation Road to the gate at the start of the loch path.'

'How long would that take?'

'Twenty minutes, perhaps.'

'Could someone follow him without him knowing?'

'No, they'd make too much noise and he'd be aware of a torch.'

'And his killer couldn't take a short cut along the street for fear of being seen. So how was he killed, and when?'

Steer said, 'Someone was waiting at the cove – someone who knew he had to come back to the island.'

115

'How did he know that?' Pagan asked of Beatrice.

Surprised, she said, 'His sleeping bag, all his gear was there. He'd lost everything else in the fire.'

'How did the killer know about his camp?'

Beatrice looked blank. Miss Pink said, 'That's easily explained. Three—' She stopped dead.

'Yes?' Pagan asked pleasantly.

'Three of us were there,' she said, without expression. 'Miss Swan, myself and Lady MacKay. We didn't keep quiet about it when we returned. After all, we thought the poor fellow was mad and had to be found. He'd set fire to his house—'

'You thought he was responsible for that?'

Beatrice said tentatively, 'There were two fires, on consecutive nights. I believe everyone thought he was responsible for the first one.'

'I still believe he was,' Miss Pink said.

'And why is that, ma'am?'

'Because that night he made no bones about returning to sleep in that place.'

'Returning from where?'

'From my house. He called on me late that night, in something of a state. That was just after his wife left him.'

Steer produced a notebook and she was taken back over that visit from Campbell, recalling her reactions which, in retrospect, were imbued with something of fantasy themselves – her fears for Debbie and the children, her inability to distinguish fact from fantasy. Campbell had said his family had gone, he said the fire had been set in order to burn his records, that he would dust for prints, that he possessed those of all the locals, collected over the years. . . . Pagan interrupted. 'He said that: "all the locals"?'

'Why, yes.'

'And on the second night' – he transferred his gaze to Beatrice – 'he shouted "I've got your prints" at the intruder.'

Miss Pink looked at her friend, thinking furiously. Steer turned back the pages in his notebook. Beatrice said slowly, 'I remember fingerprints were mentioned but . . . ' She spread her hands helplessly and Miss Pink felt a twinge of anxiety; she was too old and frail for horror at this hour of the night, at any time. 'Can't we continue this in the morning?' she pleaded. 'We'll be much better after a night's sleep.'

Pagan was all apologies. Steer made to close his notebook, but his superior stopped him with a gesture. 'We'll spare you the questions,' he told them. 'Listen to the sergeant for a moment and tell us if he's got it right.'

Steer cleared his throat and started to read in his Glaswegian accent: 'Campbell was knocked to the ground but not rendered unconscious. He went outside and saw the intruder running fast into the trees. Intruder wore a hood but no gloves. Campbell shouted: "I have you now. You have left your fingerprints." Campbell continued conversation with information on the science of fingerprints which sounded authoritative.'

Pagan lifted a hand and Steer, who had read the last sentence with difficulty, stopped. 'Is that correct?' Pagan asked.

Beatrice was puzzled. 'I don't remember his talking about the science of fingerprints.' She looked at Miss Pink, who said, 'It's near enough what he told us. I gather those notes were taken from customers who were in the bar on the night of the big fire.'

Beatrice gave them her sweet smile. 'Of course, you've been talking to other people.'

'So,' Pagan went on, 'evidently the fire was set to destroy the prints. Whether or not Campbell did collect fingerprints, someone believed he did, and that was the same person who broke in before the fire – trying to find out if Campbell kept records on local people. This chap didn't believe the fantasy about secret agents, of course, but he did know that Campbell was inquisitive and mad enough to follow any interesting trail that presented itself – like petty thieves who wear gloves.'

Miss Pink, who had been following this carefully despite her fatigue, interrupted: 'No, he wasn't wearing gloves.'

'The thefts from cars back in the summer.'

They stared at him. 'Go on,' Miss Pink said.

'Only two of those cars were printed. People were too busy to attend to the others. Thefts from cars in the summer run into hundreds. Where those two cars were concerned, the thief wore gloves. Legitimate prints were smudged. And all the burglarised

117

cars were Renault 14s or Ford Sierras of particular years, if they weren't unlocked. The thief had keys. What does that say to you?'

'He didn't have any work to do,' Miss Pink said promptly. 'He didn't have to pick a lock or break a window—' Her voice trailed away.

'Only money was taken; no cameras or clothes, no credit cards, only money – and that can't be traced in the normal way. What kind of chap likes cash but doesn't know a fence, won't risk obtaining money on a credit card, and wears gloves?'

'It sounds like Campbell,' Miss Pink said. 'Immature, an opportunist, careful – but it couldn't have been. He was killed.'

'The point is,' Pagan said, as if he hadn't heard, 'there were two arsonists, but only one matters. Campbell set the first fire out of pique because his wife walked out. She'd had enough when he told her he'd been recruited by MI6 before he met her. We got that by way of the Pitlochry people,' he added, seeing Miss Pink's amazement. 'But the second fire was for real – and petrol bombs were used; the firemen found the bottles. And Campbell came straight to you. Why?'

Miss Pink's eyelids were drooping. 'He told us about the fire. . . . ' Her words seemed distant, ' . . . the intruder, finger-prints . . . He wouldn't go home – he had no home. We didn't believe him. He asked for a gun and Miss Swan refused. That's why he came – for a gun.'

'He came here?'

'No, to my house. Miss Swan was dining with me.'

'And did you give him a gun, ma'am?'

Beatrice stared at him. 'Of course not. I feel bad about it.'

'He could have done a lot of damage.'

'I mean, I feel bad because I didn't take him seriously.'

Pagan stood up. 'It's ironic when you come to think of it. Here's this fellow, spends the greater part of his life acting a big macho role, and then he comes up against the real thing and he's snuffed out like a candle.'

Chapter 11

Gales lashed the coast throughout the night. The loch was partly sheltered by the southern headland, but last evening when Pagan dropped her at her door Miss Pink tasted salt on her face. Rain and spray gleamed in the lights, merging and parting in drifts of grey and gold. The sweep of water on tarmac was punctuated by waves crashing on the shore.

With her window closed she slept badly, waking in the small hours to become aware that the sea was quieter, but the wind howled like a wolf in the power lines. Savage gusts drove fistfuls of rain against the window panes. A continuous low note puzzled her until she identified it as the roar of the open ocean.

She slept soundly then and woke at nine to a wet and windy morning with the cloud ceiling skimming the escarpment. Waterfalls draped the crags like shreds of lace, obscured even as she watched by a mass of rain.

By nine-thirty an increased volume of traffic in the street was noticeable; by ten the shop was so busy that cars were parked outside her sitting-room window, obstructing the view. Whenever there was a lull in the weather, people with video equipment and movie cameras appeared on the turf across the way.

Beatrice telephoned. 'Are you alone?' she asked. 'I thought you might have company with all the traffic about. Is this the Press or police?'

'I imagine it's the Press. They seem to be concentrating on the Millars.'

'Poor Rose – I must go, there's someone at the door. I'll call you back.'

Miss Pink put down the receiver and moved to the window, looking over the net that draped its lower half and glowering at a battered station wagon. She glanced at her typescript, waiting for the telephone to ring. After a few minutes she guessed that

119

the visitors had remained at Feartag and applied herself to the chore of answering her agent's letter about a Brazilian edition of her current book. After twenty minutes the telephone rang.

'It was the police,' Beatrice said. 'They wanted to see Robert's guns – to make sure they hadn't been "interfered with", they said. Could they be implying that I'm so old I wouldn't notice someone had been in my bedroom and broken into the cabinet?'

'It's more likely they thought that the reason Campbell came to you on that last night was to borrow – or indeed to take – a gun.'

'That sounds more reasonable. But of course all the guns are there and the cabinet was locked. Melinda, they actually smelled the barrels! I told them some would have Campbell's prints on them because he was helping me clean them on Friday. But they didn't dust them – is that the term?'

'Yes. Did the results of the autopsy come through?'

'Pagan said nothing. Why?'

'I wondered if Campbell had been shot.'

'Surely not, with those injuries. Pagan was acting rather brash this morning; perhaps he's been upset by the reporters. By the way, did you tell him about my telephone calls?'

'Which . . . ? Oh, the heavy breather. Certainly not. Why?'

'He knew about them. It followed on from the guns, d'you see; he said he appreciated why I'd been shooting; it would remind the villagers that I had firearms in the house. He said: "I mean the person who was making the telephone calls." So I thought you must have told him last night.'

'Who did you tell besides me?'

'No one. But Esme had the same problem – perhaps she told them.'

'Cross-checking,' murmured Miss Pink. 'And he tricked you into revealing you'd had heavy breather calls.'

'He wanted to know who I thought was responsible. Surely Esme wouldn't have told them she suspected Hamish?'

'She made no bones about naming him to us. In fact, she maintained his activities went way beyond nuisance calls.'

'Why would he want to frighten old ladies and lonely spinsters? It doesn't make sense.'

'Perhaps the caller, whoever it was, wanted attention. Or it could have been the thrill of power, and that's heady stuff. Look how he played on your emotions, and Esme's.'

'Not to speak of his own fa—' Beatrice broke off, and resumed in a different tone, 'There's too much psychology in this for me. It started as mischief and got out of hand. I'm only glad the calls have stopped; now perhaps we can get back to our old routine.'

Miss Pink wondered if Beatrice had achieved the blinkered attitude of some old people who block out the more negative aspects of modern life, at least when not personally involved. Her telephone calls had stopped, so she was unconcerned about heavy breathers. And although she was aware of murder, the fact that the killer could be one of her neighbours seemed to have escaped her. Miss Pink suggested a drive, luncheon in Morvern or Ullapool, that she come to Feartag for coffee – all of which the old lady declined on the excuse that she was going to redecorate her guest room.

The telephone rang soon after Miss Pink replaced the receiver. It was Coline. 'I've been trying to reach you,' she said hurriedly when Miss Pink, not wanting an invitation to the lodge, said she was on her way to Morvern. Coline said this was perfect: 'I had a call from Flora. Buffy MacLean's brought her back as far as Slaggan. D'you know it – Invermarsco House, a few miles beyond Morvern? Would it be too dreary to go out of your way a mile or two and pick her up? I'd be most grateful; we've got the police here again this morning. They were here last evening too: a fellow called Pagan with his sidekick, Steer, who looked very virile; both names highly inappropriate if you ask me. They wanted to know all about the fire, among other things, and this morning the forensic people are down there sieving ashes. They wanted us on hand, but I removed myself after a while. When you've seen one sooty milk bottle you've seen them all. Did you know petrol bombs were used?'

'The smell was strong.'

'So I left Ranald there, getting under their feet. Pagan seems eager to find Hamish – almost as if they've got him labelled as a suspect. Flora's going to enjoy this.'

The drive south was wet and dismal and she would have turned back had she not agreed to act as cab driver. She passed through Morvern and the sign for Slaggan appeared on the verge. Vaguely recalling past journeys, she continued through a hamlet comprising a hotel, petrol pumps and a few houses to where, a mile beyond, stone pillars stood at the side of the road and a drive took off between sodden rhododendrons.

Invermarsco House was large, its owner slim and chipper: an elderly Don Juan who insisted on her taking a glass of sherry before starting back. Flora's big strap bag was in the hall and, thrown over a chair, a fur that looked like a wolf's skin – oddly exotic for the Highlands. As she was ushered into the drawing room MacLean shouted up the stairs, 'She's staying for sherry, Flora; come and have a Coke.'

When Flora appeared, she looked as if she hadn't changed her clothes; she was still wearing the Escada top, the baggy pants and trainers. She had a new cropped hairstyle but, despite its sophistication – perhaps because of it – she looked like a child actor playing an adult role. She was saying, 'It was too bad of Mum to ask you to pick me up.'

'I'd have run her home if I'd known,' MacLean said. 'How are they making out in Sgoradale? What's this about a chap being found drowned? Suicide, was it?'

'I told him what Campbell was like,' Flora explained. 'He reckons it's an occupational hazard if you live on the coast: losing your marbles and committing suicide.'

'It's too remote up there around Loch Sgoradale,' MacLean said. 'Foreigners can't stick it. They leave, or they stay and go ga-ga. Seen it happen scores of times.'

'Come off it, Buffy,' Flora jeered. 'Some crofters stay sane.'

'They're not foreigners.'

She sniffed and turned back to Miss Pink. 'How's Debbie taking it?'

'I really don't know.' Miss Pink went off into a spiel about Campbell's being an agent for MI6 or MI5, and Debbie's going home to her mother in Pitlochry, which MacLean received with courteous bewilderment and Flora with impatience. As soon as

122

Miss Pink put down her empty glass, the girl stood up and said it was time they were leaving. Back on the road, the car's nose turned for home, she said, 'You didn't want me to ask any more questions in there, particularly about Debbie. What happened?'

'As I said, she left Campbell. Then he set his place on fire – your mother's place, rather. Are the newspapers saying he committed suicide?'

'I haven't seen any today, and Buffy doesn't have a telly. What else could it have been?'

Miss Pink hesitated. Flora was only sixteen. Snuggled in her furs, she regarded the older woman steadily. 'Not suicide?' she ventured.

'I'm afraid he was murdered.'

'You're having me on.' Silence. 'No, you're not.' Another silence. Flora stared through the windscreen. 'Debbie?' she asked. 'Is she all right? And the kids?'

'Oh, yes. They were safely away by the time he . . . died.'

'How did he die?'

Miss Pink looked at the girl's profile. 'You've lost weight.'

'I was too fat?'

'Puppy fat, in the cheeks.'

'This is a red herring. How did Campbell die?'

'He was hit over the head, put in his boat, tied to the painter, and the boat sent to the bottom.'

Flora sighed, then breathed deeply for a few moments. 'You'd better tell me everything,' she said.

Miss Pink told her what she knew of Campbell's movements, adding a rider that, with hindsight, one couldn't tell how much of his own statements was true. 'Which may account for his downfall,' she said, and reminded Flora of his propensity for playing games. 'He could have seen something he shouldn't, something connected with a crime.'

'What kind of crime?'

'If we knew that, we'd know who the murderer is.'

'No kidding. I was talking to Neil – that's my friend's father in Edinburgh; he suggested I should go into television – as a journalist. I'd like to specialise in crime. What do you think?'

'What attracts you about criminal work?'

'People's minds, what makes them tick. OK, so Campbell was eliminated because he knew too much, but *what* did he know? It's fascinating. Are there crime reporters in the village?'

'I'm sure there are; the place is swarming with media people. Did your mother tell you about Hamish?'

'Of course, that's why I had to come home. She's going up the wall about the ponies.'

'It seems irresponsible going off when you were away, and your mother says he was paid to look after the animals.'

'He's no good without supervision.'

'Does it surprise you that he's disappeared?'

'Not really. "Disappeared"? That's an odd way of putting it.'

'How would you put it?'

'I thought he'd run away – like they do, kids, to Inverness or somewhere. You're not suggesting there's something sinister about it, are you?'

'You remember the thefts from cars in the summer?'

'Yes. What's that got to do with—'

'And the police car in the nurse's drive?'

'Oh, that!'

'And strange telephone calls: heavy breathers, and anonymous letters.'

'Those are new since I left.'

'They're not, actually. There's a feeling that Hamish may be at the bottom of it all.'

'*Hamish*? Oh, no—' Flora stopped suddenly and blinked. She started to frown. 'Hamish,' she repeated thoughtfully and then, as if she'd thought of it herself: 'It could be, you know.' She laughed. 'Rebelling against his old man? And now he's been found out and he's run away. Typical.'

Miss Pink thought about the intruder running from Campbell's cottage, and the fire, the big fire – links in a chain that ended in murder. 'Why should he steal from cars? What did he spend the money on?'

Flora looked blank. 'I've no idea. What do kids spend money on? Drink, drugs, cigarettes? I don't know what he did in the evenings with his friends.'

'He doesn't seem to have had any.'

'Are *you* investigating?' Flora twisted round in her seat. 'What fun! Can I help?'

'Not me. An inspector called Pagan's heading the investigation. I'd like to see his reaction to an offer of help from you.'

'I'm not a child.'

'Well, the new hairstyle and the furs are sophisticated enough, but you still look like a child. Are you aware of that?'

'People keep telling me. That's the point of the new image – trying to look my age.'

'Would a sixteen-year-old buy a wolfskin?'

'This is rabbit. You can get long-haired rabbit fur of any shade nowadays. Actually it's supposed to be lynx.' She looked hurt.

'I'm sorry. It looks well on you.'

They went through Morvern. On the open road again, Flora asked, 'When did he go?'

'Hamish? On Sunday night, but it was only discovered yesterday morning.' She told Flora about the dummy in the bed and the reactions of the Knoxes.'

'Didn't he leave a note or anything?'

'Evidently not. His father suggested that he was up to some comparatively harmless prank, with a gang or at least with someone who could drive, and they were stranded a long way from home – an accident perhaps. But he drew a blank with hospitals and other policemen. One can't help feeling that if Hamish doesn't communicate it's because he can't.'

'Or won't, is more like it. He's scarpered. He got cold feet when Campbell was found and he's run away because he's got a guilty conscience. He's not going to be around when the police start making enquiries about who's been playing practical jokes.'

'That makes sense except that Campbell's body was found after Hamish disappeared.'

'Well, he knew it was g—' In a tense silence she stole a glance sideways at Miss Pink whose attention was on the road, her lips pursed. 'Are you thinking what I'm thinking?' Flora asked.

'The point is: are the police thinking it? Unless Hamish

comes back soon, they're going to suspect a connection.'

'Yes, we want that lad badly.' Pagan took his cup from Miss Pink. 'He has a motive; it's an adolescent motive, but it's there.'

After dropping Flora at the lodge she had reached her cottage to find Pagan's car parked outside. She'd been indoors only long enough to make a pot of tea when he was at the door; he'd seen her arrive from Esme's sitting room, he told her. He said nothing of Steer's whereabouts. He had opened the conversation with the subject of Hamish.

'A motive for what?' she asked.

He looked pained. 'All right, you have to go through the motions' – she remembered that Beatrice had said he was brash this morning – 'but they've come clean—' His gesture implied the whole community. 'There's Miss Dunlop: a mine of information, she is, fills any gaps left by the nurse and the postmistress – and anyone else come to that.' He looked at her meaningly. 'But you're the one whose word I can rely on.'

She was on her guard immediately – but she didn't know where he'd been all day, what he'd been doing, and she'd had no time to find out. Why should she worry? Because in this small community there were a number of people she liked, and none whose arrest she might view with equanimity.

'You're quiet,' he said.

'I was waiting for your questions.'

'I'm here for discussion, not questions.'

She gave him a cat's smile; appreciative, knowing. 'Tell me what you've learned that presents Hamish with a motive.'

He answered obliquely. 'There were the phone calls, and just one solitary letter – to Miss Dunlop. You were there when she received it; she refuses to divulge its contents.'

'I suspect that it was needling her: jeering at her for a lesbian, and in obscene terms. The accusation would have shocked her to the core.'

'Enough to murder the writer?'

'Oh, come, Inspector: in these days?'

There was silence, wary on her part, thoughtful on his.

When he spoke again, he'd changed the subject. 'This boy

126

came and went as he pleased at night; there's a flat roof outside his bedroom window and the house is built into a bank. Take the time he put the police car in the nurse's drive; he'd wait until his parents were watching something noisy on television. Knox says the keys were in the car; I'd have his hide for that, but there are more important issues at stake. The nurse says Hell's Angels were responsible.' Miss Pink said nothing. 'And you?' he prompted.

'Hell's Angels wouldn't have known about village relationships. Those aren't talked about except within the family, sometimes not then.' Pagan waited. 'She thinks it was Hamish,' Miss Pink said.

'That's what Miss Dunlop told us.'

She took his empty cup without a word and held his eye as she returned it. 'Have the results of the autopsy come through?'

'I should have told you. Campbell's dentist identified him – or rather, the jaws. There was water in the lungs. He was alive when he went in the loch.'

'He didn't die of that terrible battering?'

'He would have done, the brain was a mess. We also have the results on those prints from the pans and things in the tent – Campbell's prints slightly smudged. Could be that on a cold night Campbell was wearing gloves, but you wouldn't expect it of a man who's lived here for ten years. And if he had been, his old prints would have been heavily smudged. So someone else was in the tent, and wearing gloves. Ties in with the car thief – you look serious. Something struck you there?'

'A thought hovering at the back of my mind. It's gone, but it will come back. So, gloves at the camp and the car park, but no gloves when he ran away from the cottage. Why not then as well? Will you have some more shortbread? What have I said?'

He was staring at her. '"No gloves when he ran away from the cottage",' he repeated. 'You're right. If it was the same person, why the lapse in precautions on the night of the fire? He didn't have a car either. Everything points to young Hamish.'

'Surely it's all circumstantial.'

'Not even that, ma'am; we haven't got a case. But we want him and we're going to find him. Although if he's responsible for something more than petty theft and a few naughty pranks then he's in Glasgow by now, or even further afield, like London. But he's a young lad; he doesn't know his way around. We'll find him. You look doubtful.'

'I can't get over his wearing a mask and forgetting gloves. It's inconsistent. He wiped his prints— Have you been told about the cottage that was broken into: Camas Beag?'

'Lady MacKay told us. She said you thought the place was too clean. I'll send Steer over there, but there's little point in printing it; too many people have been in since, and then there were all the visitors before. It's a pity because if he had left a print at that cottage, it could be the one that would nail him.'

'Really? What have you got to tie that intruder to anything else that's happened, least of all the murder? What puzzles me is why anyone should break into Camas Beag. The beds hadn't been slept in, no food had been taken, yet the surfaces must have been wiped because they were so clean under the broken window. So what did the intruder want?'

'There's no knowing how their minds work.'

'Who?'

'Killers, criminals, they're all mad.'

'Even madmen have motives that make sense to them.'

Chapter 12

By Wednesday morning rain had been falling for sixty hours, but Sgoradale was fortunate; with the deep cut of the river to carry off storm water there were no floods, although the river itself was an awesome sight. When the rain stopped, around eleven o'clock, it was possible to hear through the thunder of the torrent the muffled rumbling of boulders being carried down the bed. Miss Pink, looking at the amber rapids from Feartag's sitting room, swore that she could feel the house vibrating.

'It does,' Beatrice said. 'It's built on rock, so the vibrations can be felt quite distinctly. It worried the police too, and it wasn't so bad yesterday morning. Wasn't it odd that they should want to see Robert's guns?'

'I don't know what was in their minds. The autopsy didn't turn up a bullet wound. I noticed a difference in Pagan's manner when he came to me yesterday: almost conspiratorial, as if he suspected I was considering Hamish as the killer although I wasn't yet ready to admit it openly.'

'I don't know.' Beatrice spoke as if she'd been giving the matter a lot of thought. 'I'm sure he'll turn up. His nerve broke and he ran away.'

'That's what Flora says, but he ran away before the body was found.'

'But not before Campbell was murdered, if the body had been in the water for longer than a day.'

'So you have come round to thinking that Hamish was responsible. It's as well you haven't given any interviews to the Press. Do you think I might have another cup of coffee?'

'There's no milk. Come to the shop with me; I'm still very wary of the reporters. You can deal with them.'

Overnight the gale had moderated and by the time they turned into the street the wind had died to a zephyr and there were splashes of sunshine on the water. A little East Coast fishing boat was coming up the loch on the tide.

'Where's she been?' Miss Pink asked. 'She was never fishing in those gales.'

'She could have put in for shelter to some remote cove and the crew have eaten all their stores. Or maybe they have some fish they caught before the gale and need to get it to market.'

She was wrong. The first inkling they had of anything untoward was when they realised that the street was empty but the quay was a jumble of cars. 'There're a lot of people in front of the hotel,' Miss Pink said. 'What can they be doing?' The fishing boat had slowed down and was coming round to the quay. 'Those people have to be the Press,' she continued. 'So there's another story, and it must be connected with the boat. Could they have picked up someone who was in trouble?'

'There was nothing on the radio.'

They were standing on the turf in the vicinity of the police house and now Joan Knox emerged from her drive and crossed the road towards them. Her hair was uncombed, she wore a shabby brown dress and bedroom slippers. She looked at them bleakly, not returning their greeting.

'What's happening, Mrs Knox?' Beatrice asked.

'They're bringing in a body.'

'How do you know?'

She looked across the water and only her lips moved. 'The captain radioed ashore.'

'Where's Mr Knox?'

'With the others on the quay. Waiting.'

Beatrice looked from her to Miss Pink, then everyone stared across the loch, two of them refusing to speculate because they felt that Joan Knox had known all along that her son would not return of his own accord nor with the police, but in some fashion like this: coming in with the tide and caught up in a fishing net.

'How would I know?' Rose Millar said. 'All I know was the shop was full of people and suddenly they were all gone. A

130

body? It's not unusual after a big blow.' But she licked her lips and her eyes were uneasy.

'Mrs Knox seems to think it's Hamish,' Beatrice said.

Rose was very still. 'Why would she think that?'

'The captain of the boat could have said it was a boy's body.'

'Well, he could have.' Her restless hands aligned and realigned magazines on the counter. 'We shall know soon enough. Why should it be him?' A door slammed at the rear of the building and she moved towards the living quarters so fast that she knocked some tins off a shelf.

'That must have been someone going out,' Beatrice said. After a few moments they heard Alec protesting loudly, his voice punctuated by urgent muttering. 'They can't hurt him,' he was saying. 'I won't let them . . . that was him on a *horse*! Cars aren't the same; I'll keep him on the lead. He's got to have his walk. . . . How can you? You got the shop to mind, and Dad's down there anyway. . . . I always walk him at – what're you doing?' This was a rising wail. 'I don't care about them; you can't keep me a prisoner—'

Rose showed for a moment, struggling with a door-stop, then the inner door slammed on herself and Alec, if not the sound of his voice. The shop-bell rang and Esme walked in. 'Good morning.' She smiled grimly. 'Have you heard?'

'Is it anyone we know?' Beatrice asked delicately.

'I didn't hang around, but rumour says it's a boy's body.' With one accord they stared through the shop window. The East Coaster was now alongside the quay.

'How's Joan taking it? I saw you talking to her.' Getting no response, Esme gestured towards the back of the shop. 'Why's that door shut – and who's that shouting?'

'She won't let Alec out,' Beatrice said.

'Well, she wouldn't, would she?'

A telephone was ringing in the house. It stopped and after a moment or two, the door to the living quarters opened gently and Alec eased into the shop, carrying the puppy. He lifted the flap in the counter only to find his way blocked by Miss Pink. Behind him Rose appeared, flustered and fierce. 'He's not to go out,' she said quickly. 'He's not well.'

131

'You must stay in this morning, Alec,' Beatrice said pleasantly, 'because we don't want you talking to the people from the newspapers.'

'Why not?' He was sweating and he didn't look all that fit. His mother had hold of his arm, but she couldn't draw him behind the counter. The puppy whined and struggled. Beatrice looked at Miss Pink, who said, 'Because the reporters are clever and they may print things you didn't say.'

'I'll sue them.'

'Oh, great!' Esme exclaimed.

'You can't.' Miss Pink was equable. 'You could if you were poor, because then the lawyer's free; in your position the bill has to be paid by your mother. Has she got several thousand pounds to give you?'

'No.' He was dumþfounded. 'She hasn't got hundreds. Oh dear, what do I do then?'

'There's no problem; let's go in and talk about it. . . . ' She had turned him round and was edging him through the doorway as she talked. None of the others followed. He stepped into a cosy little parlour and asked her to sit down. 'Now tell me what's on your mind,' he said.

'It took the wind out of my sails,' she told Beatrice when they were outside the shop again. 'The words, the intonation were a perfect mimicry of someone: wise, kind, compassionate. After that he was a child again. He didn't know what "sue" meant any more than he would know the motive behind a reporter's questions. He'd tell them every detail of his confrontation with Hamish: the poodle's being run down, the bowl hurled out of the window. He'd probably say he meant to kill Hamish.'

'I wonder if the police have interviewed him.' Beatrice looked across the water. 'People are moving; we'd better make tracks for home. You'll stay for lunch?'

'Beatrice, you're too calm. We have to find out who it is.'

'You go then; I don't want to know.'

Miss Pink stumped down the road to her car and drove to the quay. When she reached it she got out and closed the door quietly so as not to alert the people in the crowd. She could

132

distinguish Duncan Millar, old Sinclair and Butchart from the hotel. The media men were at the front and facing them were two uniformed policemen.

She skirted the people to a point which brought her astern of the boat, with no one blocking her view. For a minute or two she saw nothing remarkable, although she could hear the click of cameras and the watchers were obviously focusing on something. Then, on the boat, two men stood up – Pagan and Steer – and conferred as they looked downwards, absorbed in some object at their feet. Pagan gave an order and several men in plain clothes went aboard. The body, wrapped in tarpaulin, was lifted ashore and carried to a trailer. The police had brought in a Mobile Incident Unit. There was a general movement towards it, the detectives and the cortège followed by the Press, Miss Pink to one side.

When he reached the steps of the trailer, Pagan stopped and turned. Reporters pushed forward. Miss Pink caught his eye and saw him frown as if puzzled by her presence, but he turned back to the reporters and the cameras and said calmly, 'The body is that of a local boy, and he's been identified as Hamish Knox. He disappeared from home on Sunday night, but it was thought that he'd left the area—'

'How did he die?'

'Are there signs of foul play?'

'Is there a connection between this death and Campbell's?'

'How old was he?'

'Where is Knox?'

He held up his hand. 'Now you know,' he chided them, 'that I can't answer any questions regarding his death until after the autopsy, and as for a connection between this and Campbell's death, we'll be considering that possibility of course. The boy was sixteen; as for his father, I would expect you to cooperate here ("as I with you" was the tacit corollary) and respect the privacy of the bereaved parents.' He caught Miss Pink's eye again, nodded towards the interior of the trailer and went inside. Other men in plain clothes emerged to watch the crowd disperse. Miss Pink mounted the steps of the trailer.

The bundle lay on the floor. Pagan said grimly, 'Well, here's a pretty kettle of fish, and no mistake.' He lifted a corner of the tarpaulin and she saw features with a familiar cast, although she wouldn't have said immediately that this was Hamish Knox because she was confused by the condition of the face. She had flinched when she saw Pagan's intention, anticipating some horror similar to Campbell's head, but the same forces had not been at work here.

The face was dark where she would have expected it to be blanched, and the skin of the forehead was rubbed, giving it the appearance of scuffed leather. The lips had a blue cast, and when she looked closer she saw that the whites of the open eyes were speckled with little dark spots. She was so astonished by this that she could only stare at Pagan.

'What do you think?' he asked.

'Those flecks in the eyes – and the blue lips – can it be asphyxia?'

'Good.' He was like a professor commenting on a student's progress. Behind him two strange men were studying papers, ostentatiously not listening. Pagan seemed to be waiting.

'He was murdered?' she asked quietly.

'We mustn't jump to conclusions.'

She wanted to shake him, but as his words sank in she saw that there was a technical problem and she responded with interest. 'Asphyxia by accident?' she wondered. 'You mean he could have choked – or drowned? Do you get those flecks in drowning? What are they called? It's like pistachio.'

'Petechial haemorrhages. I think we can turn him over since he's been tumbled about by the sea for quite a while. Give us a hand here.'

He peeled back the tarpaulin and, aided by the two junior men, eased the body on to its face. It was painfully slight; she hadn't realised what a small boy Hamish was – most obvious now because, although wearing jeans and trainers, the upper part of the trunk was bare. The waist above the shrunken cinch of the jeans was reddened with a kind of blush, but the shoulders would have been white – were still white where they weren't marked with the same kind of abrasions as those on the forehead. There were similar marks on the elbows. The body had the appearance of having been partially scrubbed with a wire brush.

Pagan felt delicately in the damp hair, looked at his fingers and straightened up. 'Slight fracture there,' he said. 'You see the abrasions, ma'am?'

'The body was carried along the bottom? That's the effect of sand and rocks, after he went in the water?'

He raised his eyebrows and gestured to the dark lumbar region below the pale shoulder blades.

'*Post mortem* staining,' she said, knowing exactly what it portended, knowing as he held her eye what he would say, and he said it: '*Post mortem* staining. The body was kept somewhere before it was put in the water. We've got a double murderer on our hands. I'm going to see Knox now; he's in the hotel with Steer, away from the Press. I need more information about this boy and somehow I don't think the father's got anything else to tell me. And the mother? Is she alone now, I wonder?'

'Miss Swan was going to ask Mary MacLeod to be with her.'

'I'm worried about tonight, about people who live on their own who may have seen something they shouldn't – like Campbell did.'

'You're sure of that? What kind of crime would be worth murdering two people for?'

'Another – old – murder? You could go on for ever. And then this place has access to foreign ports. It could be drugs, although they don't come so far north usually; Cardigan Bay is good enough for the drugs runners. Poaching? Surely not. I've no idea why these two were killed, but I'm worried. Killing gets progressively easy. Our man's not mad, not so's you'd notice, but he's unhinged. And think of all the people living alone in this place without even a dog to bark at an intruder. You might spread the word around – impress on them that they ought to get home before dark this evening, and secure all their doors and windows. And that goes for you too, ma'am.'

Miss Pink's leaving the trailer was the signal for Esme to intercept her before she could reach her car. The woman had been talking to the crew of the fishing boat. When Miss Pink dutifully passed on Pagan's warning, her reaction was careless:

'And what makes him so sure it's not one of us?'

'It could be,' Miss Pink agreed. 'But asking everyone to stay indoors after dark is tantamount to a curfew; it affects the guilty as well as those at risk. Anyone abroad could be asked his business.'

'On the excuse that he's in danger? That's a bit transparent. So how was Hamish killed?'

'He was murdered and he had a fractured skull.' Pagan had told her to say no more than that.

Esme looked puzzled. 'With that storm, it's surprising he was still in one piece. Surely a fractured skull isn't sufficient evidence to assume he was murdered? The impact could have been against a rock. What else did the police tell you?'

'Only that: a fractured skull.'

'I see. There must have been other marks, but you've been told not to talk. That way they may be able to trap the murderer and weed out false confessions from exhibitionists, right?'

'Aren't you bothered about Hamish being killed?'

'No. He was a hooligan – far worse than a gang of louts because he was a loner. His father is supposed to be upholding the law – but it wasn't illegal activities Hamish enjoyed, just immoral ones. Amoral, I should say. He was anti-social in the fullest sense of the word. He's got his come-uppance, and you ask me if I'm bothered!'

'Are you going to take that line with the Chief Inspector?'

'It's not a line; it's how I feel. Of course I shall say the same thing to him. What do I have to be afraid of?'

A car came round the Lamentation bend and turned into the nurse's drive. 'You'll have to excuse me,' Miss Pink said. 'I have to see Anne.'

'I'll come with you. I have to see her too,' Esme said firmly in the face of Miss Pink's hesitation and then, coyly: 'You can't have things all your own way, you know!'

Anne Wallace's reaction to their appearance on her doorstep was certainly not one of pleasure, although it was difficult to determine what emotion was uppermost in her mind. Her gaze flicked from one to the other, then to the quay. 'Is it important?' she asked, holding the door as if prepared to close it in their faces.

'Extremely important,' Miss Pink said.

'You'd better come in then.' There was no attempt at politeness. 'I'm in a rush this morning,' she went on, leading the way to her kitchen. 'I've just nipped in for a coffee and a bite to eat and I'm off again. Will you have coffee?'

Miss Pink declined for both of them. Esme was silent, but her eyes followed every movement of the nurse as she filled a kettle, switched it on and turned back to them. 'Well?'

'You know that Hamish's body has been recovered?' Miss Pink asked.

Anne's face was set. 'Yes?'

'Did Knox call you?' Esme asked.

Anne turned on her as if she'd been attacked. 'You mind your own business!' Her wild eyes came back to Miss Pink. 'What have they done with him?'

Panic was infectious and there was a trace of it in Esme's reaction: 'What would they do with him? He's not arrested. You're not thinking straight. He's the boy's father!'

Anne swallowed, fighting for control. She kept her eyes on Miss Pink. 'How did he come to be in the water? And what's it got to do with Gordon anyway?'

'Hamish was murdered,' Esme said coldly.

'No!' Anne looked from one to the other. 'That's her exaggeration, isn't it?' There was a smothered snort from Esme. Anne faced her. 'You talk like a bad book: always making things up. You get your kicks out of other people's lives.'

'She's right,' Miss Pink said. 'He was murdered.'

'So?' The kettle boiled, was switched off and ignored. Miss Pink told her of the fractured skull, of Pagan's warning about a double murderer, of the need for prudence.

'What kind of prudence do you employ against a homicidal maniac?' Esme asked. 'He broke into Camas Beag just by smashing a window-pane.'

'He's not a maniac,' Miss Pink said. 'And as for Camas Beag—'

'Why do you say that?' Anne was strident. 'If he's killed two people in a week, what's stopping him killing a third, or more? Why is he doing it?'

'You tell us,' Esme said.

'You interfering old cow!'

'That's enough, Esme!' Miss Pink showed a flash of anger. 'You were persecuted too; don't forget that. Whoever was playing tricks on village people had an instinct for vulnerable targets.' Esme licked her lips. Miss Pink turned back to Anne. 'It's because the police don't know the motives for the murders that Pagan wants us all to take precautions, particularly if we live alone. Being the nurse, you may be forced to go out on call. I suggest you telephone Pagan at the hotel and ask him if you can have an escort in an emergency.'

Anne gaped. 'How long is this going to last?'

'Presumably until Pagan is sure that it's safe again.'

'That's when he's caught,' Esme said savagely. 'And how long is that going to take, that's what she's saying, right?'

Accusing eyes were turned on Miss Pink – united now in their distrust of her. She was the scapegoat for a situation that confined them to houses where the enemy could effect entry just by smashing a pane of glass.

Chapter 13

She glanced across the water as she drove along the street, saw that trees obscured Camas Beag and had a sensation of *déjà vu*. At Feartag Beatrice looked up in astonishment as she burst into the kitchen. 'I know why he went to Camas Beag: to use the telephone! Three years ago someone broke into a summer cabin in Montana for the same reason. I suddenly remembered.'

'That means that the person who broke into Camas came from a house without a telephone.'

'Not necessarily. He could have had a telephone but not the opportunity to use it. Every road seems to lead back to Hamish.' She recounted her interview with Pagan; she had been circumspect with Esme and Anne, but at Feartag she felt secure and uninhibited. She told Beatrice about the petechial haemorrhages and what they meant.

'You're much more confident about this murder,' Beatrice said.

'The motive for Hamish's death seems obvious.'

'Didn't you think it was in the case of Campbell?'

'Ye-es, that he saw something he shouldn't have seen – but Hamish was alive then – that's a point. How does the sequence go? I found Campbell's body on Monday afternoon and he was here Saturday evening. With the amount of damage that had been done to the body, he must have been put in the water on Saturday night, probably not long after he left here. But Hamish was around on Sunday; he was searching for Campbell at the back of Fair Point. Hamish disappeared on Sunday night, and turns up in the sea on Wednesday morning. Where was he on Monday and Tuesday?'

Beatrice shook her head helplessly. 'I'm talking to myself,' Miss Pink said. 'The autopsy may be able to narrow down the time of death – the extent to which his last meal was digested and so on – but if we assume he climbed out of his bedroom

139

window some time around . . . tennish? There's a huge gap before he was put in the sea, and that was either Monday night or last night.'

'How do you arrive at that?'

'Because the trawler picked up the body at the mouth of the loch, and it had to be put in the water on an ebb tide. The tide turned last night around eleven.'

'You left out Sunday. If he left his home about ten in the evening, the tide would be ebbing until about three in the morning.'

Miss Pink was silent. When she did speak her mind was elsewhere; she said absently, 'He wasn't put in the sea the first night.' Her eyes glazed. 'Yes,' she said at last, 'he could have been put in the water anywhere on an ebb tide, even from the lighthouse road, and he'd still be found at the mouth of the loch.' She focused suddenly on Beatrice. 'I'll opt for last night,' she said crisply. 'There was a risk of his coming back on a rising tide otherwise.'

'Why are you so sure it wasn't the first night?'

'The body was kept on land for over eight hours.' She explained about *post mortem* staining. 'The blood drains downward after death so that, if a body is on its back as this one was, the dorsal parts are stained, but not those parts that are in contact with the ground, like shoulders. After six to eight hours, the blood coagulates and if the body is then moved, the blood can't disperse, so you know whether a body has been kept elsewhere before discovery.'

'That's amazing. Are you saying that the person who strangled Hamish kept the body for two days – in the *village*?'

'The village, or a car, a boat, a byre, even a ruin. All traces of where it was kept would have been washed away by the sea. He wasn't strangled by the way; there were no marks on the throat. He was suffocated.' Beatrice looked stricken. 'Sorry,' Miss Pink muttered absently. After a while she asked, 'Why would he want to use a telephone?'

Beatrice treated this as rhetorical until the silence seemed to demand an answer. 'How could I know, Melinda? He had to speak to someone of course, and he needed privacy.'

140

'And when did he call?' Miss Pink asked, and then answered her own question: 'It was before our visit to Camas Beag – which was on the Saturday. Campbell's cottage was set on fire Friday night.' She regarded Beatrice so intently that the older woman began to fidget. 'Campbell visited you on the Saturday evening,' she said, 'and you kept something back . . . '

'No—'

'Campbell recognised Hamish—'

'He didn't say—'

' . . . as the intruder who ran away from the cottage earlier that evening, the person who knocked him down.'

'The intruder wore a hood.'

'But he wasn't wearing gloves.'

'He forgot his gloves.'

'He wore a hood and forgot gloves? Rubbish. How did Campbell know it was a man – or a boy?'

'The figure,' Beatrice said wildly. 'He was slight, like a—'

'Like a boy. Men aren't slight. It was Hamish and he wasn't wearing a hood.'

Beatrice looked so miserable that Miss Pink went to the sitting room and returned with a bottle of Cointreau. 'Can't find your brandy,' she said, pouring a generous measure into a glass. 'You can't hurt Hamish now,' she went on gently. 'Nor Campbell. In any event, you can tell me.'

'There's a problem.' Beatrice shook her head: an old lady close to the end of her tether. 'I can tell you what Campbell said, but you know how much reliance can be placed on that.'

'So that's it! You didn't say anything before because you didn't believe it.'

Beatrice nodded eagerly. 'Campbell seemed to be acting in character – hysterical, making wild accusations. . . . Yes, he did say he lied to us about the intruder wearing a hood; that in fact he wasn't, and that although he was running away so he didn't see the face, he knew it was Hamish by his figure and his agility. I didn't put any credence on it. I thought he was accusing someone who was hostile to him – just another example of paranoia – if that was—'

Miss Pink interrupted. 'Why was Hamish hostile to Campbell?'

141

Beatrice frowned, trying to remember a conversation four days old. 'He showed no surprise that Hamish was the intruder, nor that he'd turned violent. . . . And he was quite sure that Hamish was the arsonist—'

'Hamish's speciality was practical jokes,' Miss Pink mused. 'He didn't try heavy breather calls here because Campbell had no phone. Anonymous letters? Somehow Campbell doesn't seem a suitable target. He might have known something about the police car being put in Anne's drive . . . cars! His cottage was close to the car park; could he have seen Hamish breaking into vehicles back in the summer?'

'It's a possibility—'

Miss Pink rushed on, 'You wouldn't think anyone would murder for that – although children murder for the most trivial motives.' Beatrice gaped at her. She went on, 'Someone postulated a gang from outside – Hell's Angels – but what about a local gang? No, too risky, too many people involved – but someone telephoned from Camas Beag after the fire. The sequence was: fire, telephone call, Campbell killed, Hamish killed. Doesn't it look as if Campbell was murdered because he knew too much, then Hamish because he could expose Campbell's killer?'

'Campbell was murdered just because he knew Hamish had been stealing from cars?'

The question hung between them and they were so absorbed by it that for a moment neither could identify a familiar sound from the passage.

'Telephone,' Beatrice murmured. As she stood up, someone pounded the door knocker.

'I'll see to that,' Miss Pink said.

Pagan was on the doorstep. She was annoyed at the interruption. 'You're operating alone again. Short-handed?'

'Always. May I come in?'

Beatrice nodded a greeting to him as she listened to her caller on the telephone. Miss Pink took him along the passage to the sitting room and offered coffee. He declined. 'I'll get caffeine poisoning. People are hurt if I refuse, but with you I can be truthful. I can't take any more coffee.'

'You've had a hard morning?'

He sighed. 'Did you pass on my warning? Good. And did you learn anything from Miss Dunlop and the nurse?'

'Not really. Esme Dunlop is convinced Hamish asked for trouble. They're both concerned that a killer's on the loose. The nurse is worried about Gordon Knox. Did he say anything about the odd incidents – like the police car in the nurse's drive?'

'He suspected Hamish all along but he couldn't tackle the boy, or was afraid to. He's not the first officer to sow a wild oat in middle age, but he says he didn't intend it to become serious. He's probably speaking the truth. The nurse is a trifle long in the tooth – a bit possessive, if you take my meaning.'

'Making allowances for the chauvinist attitude, I do. Is that significant, that the relationship was one-sided?'

'That depends. Would you say that the nurse is unbalanced?'

'No. Infatuated, perhaps; I'd leave it at that.'

He stood up as Beatrice entered, flustered because he wasn't taking any refreshment, thinking it had not been offered. Having got that straight, she asked diffidently if he had come for another interview. Pagan said he was just passing, and turned back to Miss Pink. 'Have you thought of anything I should know?'

She looked meaningly at Beatrice who blinked, refusing her cue. Miss Pink spoke for her. 'Campbell said he recognised Hamish as the intruder at his cottage.' Pagan listened without comment as she elaborated, but halfway through the explanation she said petulantly, 'This doesn't surprise you.'

'No, ma'am. We knew enough about the so-called practical jokes and about young Hamish to have him down as a suspect for that fire.'

'And did you suspect that it was Hamish who broke into Camas Beag to phone an accomplice after the fire – and before Campbell was murdered?'

'No,' Pagan said slowly. 'I hadn't thought of that. An accomplice – to what?'

'Well, we were saying,' Beatrice put in chattily, 'would

143

Campbell be murdered just because he'd seen Hamish break into a car?'

'No, but if something more than theft was involved . . . ' Pagan left that hanging and reverted to the accomplice. 'So you reckon this other person wasn't in the neighbourhood?'

'Do we?' Miss Pink asked. 'We hadn't speculated.'

'He made a telephone call after the fire and before Campbell was killed,' Pagan repeated. 'Was he asking for advice – or orders? Or bringing in his accomplice? That boy couldn't have overpowered a grown man, surely?'

'Oh, no.' Beatrice was firm. 'Campbell didn't look strong but he was wiry, and much heavier than a boy of course.'

'He brought in an accomplice from elsewhere,' Pagan mused. 'Yet another point in young Alec's favour.'

They stared at him. Miss Pink laughed. 'You haven't been interviewing Alec!'

'The whole family. It was hard work, but I think we got the picture quicker than if we'd taken them separately. Alec says in all seriousness that he'd intended to kill Hamish but he changed his mind. His mother thinks he's accusing himself – virtually confessing – and tells a lie every time she speaks, to be contradicted by Alec immediately. The father walked out after five minutes.'

'Good.' Miss Pink's tone was absent. 'This business is far too sophisticated for Alec.'

'What business?' Beatrice asked.

Miss Pink looked at Pagan. 'Well, what is it? What's the crime behind the murders, the motive for them? You must have considered possibilities, however remote.'

'I'll leave that to you ladies.' He was trying to sound gallant. 'Your minds are fertile enough. Me, I'm working from the other end. I've got two bodies; I'm trying to discover who struck the final blows to each, and where Hamish's body was kept until it was put in the sea last night, on an ebb tide. At any other time, it would have come back.'

The ladies refrained from looking at each other. 'When do you expect the results of the second autopsy?' Miss Pink asked.

'Soon, ma'am; a preliminary report, anyway. The body was

144

flown out from Morvern. But I'm not expecting a lot from that direction. A rough time of death possibly; we know he had a hamburger at nine o'clock, but as for where the body was kept between whiles, I doubt those rough seas will have washed away every trace.'

After he'd gone, they stood on the gravelled sweep enjoying the bliss of soft air and sunshine after the gales.

'Lovely walking weather,' Beatrice said wistfully.

'Why not?' Miss Pink was suddenly forceful. 'There can't be any risk in broad daylight with two of us. Let's stroll along the lighthouse road.'

'Lovely. We have time. That was Coline on the telephone. She wants us to eat there tonight; a council of war, she says.'

'What's she got in mind?'

'Obviously the same subject as all of us, but it will be interesting to have a fresh light on it. You're looking doubtful. Oh, I see; we shall be out after dark.'

'I hadn't got that far; what I was thinking is that we still have no idea who killed Hamish.'

'He could be here, in Sgoradale – still?'

Miss Pink sighed at such innocence. 'He could be at the lodge.'

'That's in poor taste, Melinda.'

'So were the murders.'

Before those faded old eyes Miss Pink conceded defeat. 'I'll pick you up and bring you home,' she said. 'And we'll drive with locked doors. Even Pagan can't object to that.'

That afternoon the sky was clear of clouds and the sun was warm. 'We'll have a frost tonight,' Beatrice said as they crossed the bridge.

Miss Pink sniffed the air and agreed. They entered the North Wood, which was curiously light now that the storms had stripped much of the foliage. Sky showed through slim trunks of birch and ash and as they reached the first little house, hens were scratching for worms on the muddy verge. A plume of smoke rose from a chimney. It was all refreshingly pastoral, a blessed relief after the violence – human and elemental – of the last few days. Beyond the house they heard laughter and, looking up, saw two riders dashing across the wooded slope. A man shouted, there was a shriek; in quick succession the horses leapt an unseen obstacle and raced on.

Miss Pink was astonished. 'They're on a track,' Beatrice said.

'That has to be Flora, but who's the man?'

'It's certainly not Ranald; he can't ride like that.'

'Are there guests at the lodge?'

'Coline didn't say so. Could it be one of those reporters?'

'It could be. Flora's capable of fraternising with anyone.'

It wasn't a reporter, but the police. Towards the end of the afternoon they were returning from the lighthouse when they heard the beat of hooves approaching fast, and they spun round to halt as the riders bore down on them. They pulled up, holding their excited horses with ease: Flora and Detective Sergeant Steer.

Miss Pink was totally at a loss. Beatrice said, 'How nice to see you home again, Flora. And you've got Mr Steer to help you with the exercising.'

'He's investigating,' Flora said. 'He has to go all over the place; we've been to Lone, Fair Point, all the ruins, and now it's Camas Beag. I'm his guide; he couldn't get to those places without a horse, and couldn't find them without me.' She glanced at Steer, then studied his mount. 'We'll have to go slow,' she said. 'We're getting close to home and he's sweating like a pig.'

Steer nodded, watching her, ignoring the ladies.

'Where did you learn to ride?' Miss Pink asked.

He switched his attention with an effort. 'My dad was a stud groom, ma'am. We lived on the premises. I was brought up with horses.'

'He's mad,' Flora said. 'He thinks he's on a hunter. He'd be jumping walls if I didn't stop him.' Steer blinked lazily. 'Wouldn't you?' she pressed. His lips moved, sketching a smile. Flora held the look a moment longer and said casually but with a sigh, as if they were children obeying the grown-ups' orders, 'So now it's Camas Beag. Hamish called me one night when I was in Edinburgh and I reckon he made the call from there.'

'Called *you*?' Miss Pink repeated stupidly.

'Well, he couldn't tell anyone else, was how he put it. He'd fired the keeper's cottage. Talk about going over the top!'

'You didn't mention this when I brought you home from Buffy MacLean's place.'

'I didn't know, did I? All I knew was he'd been caught red-handed, left his prints behind and had had to burn the place down. I wasn't going to shop him. Now he's been murdered, so there's no more point in protecting him. Might as well tell the fuzz, make a clean breast of it.' She looked defiantly at Steer. 'Wouldn't have told you in the ordinary way.'

Steer grinned weakly. Miss Pink stared at him.

'Why did Hamish turn to you?' Beatrice asked Flora.

'He needed someone to intercede with Mum, I guess – and I was by way of being his employer.'

'How did he find your telephone number?' Miss Pink asked.

'He knew who I was staying with. Neil Fleming's a famous criminal lawyer and everyone knows I went to school with his daughter.'

Steer glanced at his watch. 'We'd better get on to this cottage,' he said uneasily.

'Ride on,' Flora directed. 'I'll catch you up.'

When he was out of earshot Miss Pink said, 'You've seduced that poor fellow.'

'In a manner of speaking,' Beatrice added.

Flora looked after him, wrinkling her nose. 'He's a bit rough, but there's room for improvement. Did I say something I shouldn't? Of course, I know Pagan sent him with me so's he could pump me. Did I give anything away?'

'Go on as you are,' Miss Pink said. 'You're doing fine. By the way, how long had you known that Hamish was the car thief?'

'Not till he phoned me; didn't I say? I don't think it ever crossed my mind that it could be him. He didn't need the money; there's nothing to spend it on in Sgoradale and he never went anywhere. Perhaps he was saving up for something.' She gathered her reins. 'Are you coming to our place tonight? Mum said something.'

'Flora!' She checked as Miss Pink stepped forward. 'What's Steer been doing this afternoon?'

'"Following the victim's movements," he says. And trying to find out where the body was kept.' Flora looked across the loch with a face like flint. 'I'm interested in that too.' The pony leapt away down the grass verge, flying over drainage ditches – Flora sitting like a centaur, collecting Steer as she went.

'She'll bring them home steaming,' Beatrice said with disapproval. 'That young man's head over heels in love. Isn't that an odd thing to happen?'

'Policemen are human. Look at Knox – and Flora is in a different league from Anne Wallace.'

'But Steer is supposed to be investigating a murder.'

'Violent death can be an aphrodisiac, or so I've heard.' They were walking again, Miss Pink staring at the ground. After a few minutes Beatrice asked what she was thinking.

'I was wondering if she was speaking the truth when she implied that Hamish wanted her to intercede with her mother. It seems more likely he'd be asking her for something tangible, like money.' She was silent for a few moments and when she spoke again she had changed gear. 'I wonder if he could have killed Campbell on his own after all? Although we mustn't forget that the fact that he *wasn't* phoning an accomplice from Camas Beag doesn't mean he didn't have one.'

'If he did, why didn't he confide in that person instead of phoning Flora?'

'Because Flora had money, or access to money? Because his accomplice didn't have any, or wouldn't part with it?'

'Why should Flora part with it?'

'You mean, why should he think Flora would let him have money.'

'All that is hypothetical. Flora didn't mention money.'

'You're enjoying this,' Miss Pink said, smiling. 'You're getting involved.'

'Only intellectually. I find it stimulating.'

'Then keep your eyes and ears open tonight. We might, as the lawyers say, hear something to our advantage.'

Chapter 14

By six o'clock the sun had set and the sky beyond the mouth of the loch held a pearly sheen smudged with rose. Across the shimmering water a line of cormorants hurried to their roosts on the islands.

'What about Mary MacLeod?' Beatrice asked as they drove along the street. 'Is she alone tonight?'

'I doubt it.' Miss Pink braked for a strolling cat. 'She'll be with the Millars or old Sinclair. But she's not in danger.'

'What makes you so sure of that?'

'The murders were connected with the practical jokes. Mary had none played on her.'

'So far as you know. And I thought we were agreed that knowledge of the car thefts – which weren't jokes – was insufficient motive for murder.'

'There was a connection.'

As they came up the drive the tower showed in the headlights; the forecourt was empty of cars. The family was gathered in the drawing room; everyone had dressed for dinner but no one looked dressy and the group had an air of sombre respectability.

'How are the Knoxes bearing up?' Ranald asked, bringing sherry to the guests.

'There's no way of knowing,' Beatrice said. 'All our information comes by way of the police, and Flora will have more from that source.'

'They're coming up for drinks,' Flora said.

'Pagan and Steer?' Miss Pink couldn't hide her surprise.

'I invited Steer,' Flora explained, 'and he was uneasy about accepting, so I said to bring his boss as well.'

'Common courtesy,' Coline said. 'We should set an example. Haven't you had them along for drinks?'

'One asks them to have a drink if they're there,' Beatrice

149

said, 'but is it etiquette to issue a formal invitation to men investigating a murder? It could be thought that you wanted something from them.'

'I do,' Flora said. 'Steer's going to be useful with the ponies.' Seeing their expressions, she shifted ground. 'OK, he told me what's happening. It's wild! Not just this case, but all the cases he's worked on. My mind's made up, Melinda; I'm definitely going to be a crime reporter.'

'It's rewarding to find someone who knows what she wants,' Miss Pink said. 'And what conclusions have you – and they – come to about this crime?'

She looked solemn. 'There's evidence to suggest a connection between the deaths—'

'That's more than obvious,' Ranald barked. 'We've got a multiple murderer! I keep telling you—'

'Obviously Hamish murdered Campbell,' Flora said loudly, overriding him. 'It had to be him because he didn't know enough about the tides to sink the body where it would still be submerged at low water. A local, born and bred, would have known.'

'That's a point,' Miss Pink conceded. 'And how did he lure Campbell back from the island?'

'I'm sorry, I'm not with you.'

'Campbell was about to eat his supper. The body and the boat were sunk just off the mainland shore. What was so urgent that he went ashore leaving his spoon in the beans?'

'And why weren't his fingerprints on the dixies?' Beatrice asked.

'Well, let's say that Campbell never went to the island, that Hamish was stalking him as he walked to the cove – we know someone did follow him – and Campbell was killed before he reached his boat. Then Hamish rowed to the island and set up the interrupted supper scenario, came back and scuttled the boat with the body attached.'

'What would be the purpose of the *Marie Celeste* bit?' Coline asked.

'Hamish wanted people to think that Campbell did go back to the island.'

'Why?' Ranald asked.

No one answered him. He got out of his chair and went round the circle, filling their glasses.

'Something to do with an alibi?' Coline ventured. 'To do with times?'

'He hadn't intended Campbell's body to be found?' Miss Pink wondered.

'If we'd only discovered the tent,' Beatrice said slowly, 'and the abandoned supper, and Campbell's body had remained submerged, had never been found, wouldn't we have assumed that he'd capsized during the storm and been drowned by accident?'

'Well, no,' Miss Pink countered, 'because the tent was found before the storm.'

'But the body needn't have been! If you hadn't taken it into your head to stroll along the southern shore at low water and then hung around sheltering from a shower, you'd never have seen it. Even then at first you thought the hand was weed.'

'But we'd have gone back to the island to find out if he'd revisited the tent.'

'Not necessarily before the storm. We were intended to think that Campbell drowned by accident. Or suicide: we thought that at first.'

Miss Pink regarded her friend thoughtfully. Coline said, 'This means we haven't got a double killer, but two killers. That's worse.'

'One of them's dead,' Flora said.

'But who killed Hamish?' Ranald asked.

'The investigation bifurcates at this point.' Flora grinned, enjoying her own pomposity. 'Either you say that Hamish was running a scam with someone else and that person killed Hamish because the boy was a threat in some way; or Campbell was killed by this other guy after all, and again Hamish had to be killed because he could expose the killer. That way you come back to the theory of the double murderer.'

'Which do the police favour?' Miss Pink asked.

Beatrice said quietly, 'If Hamish was killed because he could expose his partner, why did the partner allow a whole day to elapse before silencing him? Hamish could have talked to anyone during that time; he was free to come and go as he pleased. Why wasn't he killed at the same time as Campbell?'

'I can answer that one,' Ranald put in. 'When he saw this fellow – X, he's called usually – saw him take a swing at Campbell, he got the wind up and took to his heels. Murderer couldn't catch him, see?'

'He had all night and the next day in which to find Hamish,' Beatrice persisted.

'Found him, didn't he?' Ranald blared in triumph. 'Found him the next night and silenced him for good.'

'And kept him – where?' Flora asked. 'The body was kept under cover for two days.'

'Under cover?' Beatrice repeated.

'And carefully concealed. You were searching for it, for heaven's sake!'

'We weren't,' Miss Pink said. 'It was thought he'd run away.' She turned to Ranald. 'And if you're right in thinking the murderer found Hamish the following night, what made Hamish leave his bed? There was no sign of anything other than a voluntary exit, you know: the dummy in the bed, the absence of noise—'

There was a knock at the front door. 'That will be the police,' Coline said, and laughed at her own words. 'How ominous that sounds!'

Pagan and Steer had brought good suits to Sgoradale. Changed, bathed and smelling of after-shave, they made an exotic addition to the party. Far from merging with their environment, they stood out against it: stiff, smart, even handsome. Given that Steer found it difficult to keep his eyes off Flora, these two men were still the experts; side by side on a sofa, Miss Pink and Beatrice sat like embattled Buddhas – observing, listening, correlating and at first saying nothing.

'We were trying to solve the case for you,' Coline said brightly as the new arrivals accepted whisky.

'Oh, come,' Ranald protested. 'It was all hypothesis.'

'Well, not quite,' Flora murmured, and Steer's eyes came round to her as if drawn by a magnet.

'And you have no forensic evidence, sir,' came Pagan's response. 'Let alone the autopsy reports.'

Miss Pink and Beatrice sat up, Ranald gaped, Coline frowned. Flora's eyes sparkled until she remembered that Hamish was a kind of employee and carefully smoothed out her expression.

Pagan glanced at Miss Pink. 'Not much in the way of surprises externally,' he said. 'We knew about the *post mortem* staining, of course, and the depressed fracture of the skull; not enough to cause death incidentally, and delivered with a piece of wood. Not a cudgel or a club, more like the branch of a tree; there was a splinter caught in a crack of the bone – the only thing the sea left for us. Externally, that is.' He stopped talking and was met by silence. A log shifted in the fire and a few sparks flew up the chimney. 'Internally,' he went on, 'was another matter. He was full of alcohol.'

After some moments Flora said, 'He didn't drink.'

Pagan ignored her. 'He was given a lot to drink, hit on the side of the head and suffocated.'

Ranald spoke first. 'He couldn't have been in the bar, or Butchart would have talked. He must have been in someone's house.'

'Where would he go?' Pagan asked.

'*I* don't know.' Ranald was blustering.

'It doesn't have to be someone's house,' Coline said. 'He could have broken into a holiday cottage, taking a bottle with him. That could be why he went to Camas Beag originally; we never thought of that.'

'Wrong night,' Flora said. 'I told you, he called me from Camas Beag and that was two nights before he was killed.'

'He didn't have to be in a house,' Steer said. 'He could have been sat in a hayloft, or even in the open, drinking with a friend – or someone he thought was a friend.'

'Did he ask you for money?' Pagan asked sharply.

'Me?' Flora was startled, then she gave the question thought. 'He was kind of rambling; well, more than that, almost incoherent. All I could make out was that Campbell was on to him – his words: "He's on to me," – and he burned the place down to destroy his prints.'

153

'Go on, sweetie,' Coline urged. 'He asked you if the place was insured; he wasn't all that incoherent.'

'He had lucid moments, but on the whole he wasn't thinking straight – although he did say he wouldn't come to Edinburgh, that he'd go to Glasgow.'

'You didn't say that before,' Pagan said.

'It's not important. He was always talking about leaving home.'

Pagan nodded. 'His father hinted as much. What would he need in order to leave?'

'Sorry?' Flora looked blank.

'How much money would he need?'

'I've no idea.'

'You don't know much about this lad. He had over six hundred pounds under the lining of a drawer in his bedroom.'

Flora was surprised, but all she said was, 'There are good pickings in tourists' cars.'

'That's a hell of a lot of cash for a boy to have in his possession,' Ranald pointed out, 'even if he was a delinquent. What does Knox have to say about it?'

Pagan looked tired. 'The same kind of thing any parent would say who suddenly discovers he's got a delinquent son.'

In the ensuing silence Miss Pink caught the sound of voices outside the door. Flora had heard them too. She said quickly to her mother, 'I asked them up for drinks since we were having a party.'

Despite her surprise, Coline had her expression under control as Esme and Anne Wallace came in – Esme determinedly jolly, the nurse diffident, if not tense. In the resulting bustle, Miss Pink stood up and crossed the room to Pagan. 'This isn't following your advice about security,' she told him.

'On the contrary, ma'am; while they're here, they can't get into trouble.'

Her eyes flickered. 'He's in this room? Silly question, there's only Sir Ranald. *She* is in the room? Oh, come now, it could have been anyone from outside the district, or any villager.'

Pagan smiled. 'You misunderstand me. When I said these

people can't get into trouble I meant that, while under my eye, there's no danger of their becoming victims.'

'And I walked straight into the trap. You're a devious man, Mr Pagan.' She looked towards Steer, who had settled on a window seat beside Flora. They were staring at the room with unseeing eyes, their lips moving in a private conversation. 'What interpretation do you put on Hamish's being drunk?' she asked.

'He was easier to kill.'

'Is there any clue as to where his body was kept?'

He shook his head. 'Not even of where he was killed. Only the splinter in the skull. It didn't have to be a branch; it could have been a log. Everybody burns logs.' Their eyes went to the wood basket beside the fire. 'Whether there are two killers or one is immaterial,' he murmured.

It was a moment before the last statement penetrated her brain. 'Say that again.'

'If Hamish didn't help with Campbell's murder, he was there; that's why he had to be killed. I'm looking for the person who killed Hamish; once he's found, the other murder will slot into place.'

Ranald had approached. 'What you have to do,' he told Pagan, 'is find out where the body was kept—'

Miss Pink drifted away, finding Esme and Anne Wallace in a huddle with Beatrice. Across a space of carpet behind them, Flora was listening to Steer's low murmur.

The cool, clear voice of Beatrice was audible for some distance: ' . . . only in its broadest sense, Esme; by sex, I meant no more than relationships between the sexes.'

Anne Wallace said tightly, 'You're saying the motive was sexual?'

'She said she didn't—'

'I didn't make—'

Esme deferred to Beatrice, who started again. 'I didn't make myself clear, I'm afraid; I was thinking that there were few crimes without any sexual *angle*. I'm not suggesting the poor boy was killed for a sexual motive; that would be quite bizarre, even if . . . ' Aware that this part of the room had fallen silent,

155

that Steer and Flora were staring at her, she bit her lip.

Esme asked ominously, 'Even if what?'

Beatrice lowered her voice. Miss Pink pressed closer. 'Even if he wasn't normal.' The old lady looked from Esme to Anne. 'You know that,' she said.

'Know what?' Anne asked. 'All I know was that he was a juvenile delinquent, and heading for trouble.'

Miss Pink saw that Steer's interest was divided between the conversation and that part of the room where Pagan was still talking to Ranald.

'He was already in trouble,' Beatrice said. 'He always would be, given his tendencies.'

Esme's eyes were slitted. 'Are you saying he was gay?'

Anne's reaction was a whisper. 'I don't believe it!'

Beatrice addressed Miss Pink. 'It accounts for everything – including the streaker, so-called.'

'What streaker?' Several people spoke at the same time. Steer stood up, followed by Flora. Beatrice said, 'The naked man who couldn't get into his car. He ran away and found a bin liner to cover himself – he stole it from Campbell's cottage, and probably Campbell saw him. Campbell knew what was going on anyway. Why didn't that man go to the police and report that his clothes, his keys, almost certainly his wallet had been stolen? Why did he take his clothes off in the first place? We all know why people do that, and it's not usually a crime. But Hamish was under age.'

Their silence was stunned and their attitudes so stiff that Pagan, becoming aware of something untoward, started to make his way across the room. Flora was staring at Beatrice with wide eyes, smiling incredulously.

Miss Pink said, 'Is that anything more than a hypothesis?'

Beatrice sighed. Steer intercepted Pagan and spoke quietly. Flora looked from the police to Beatrice with the absorbed air of a child.

Pagan advanced. 'Tell me about this naked man, ma'am.'

Beatrice shook her head. Things had got out of hand, she implied. 'Village gossip. I know nothing more than anyone else. I just remembered, that's all. Everyone else had forgotten.'

Coline and Ranald approached and the other residents hastened to enlighten him, delighted to find something he hadn't known – something which he obviously found important. Miss Pink hovered on the edge of the group, listening to them trying to cap each other's stories concerning that hitherto forgotten incident. After a while, she became aware that her feet were aching and was reminded that she'd walked a considerable distance today. Looking round for a comfortable seat, she saw that Flora and Beatrice had retreated to a sofa where they were absorbed in conversation – Flora pensive, Beatrice talking with animation. They were discussing wildlife: "badger", Miss Pink caught, and "Kenya".

'Kenya?' she repeated, subsiding in an easy chair. 'What's this?'

Flora blinked at the interruption, even Beatrice looked a trifle disconcerted. Miss Pink realised that she could have drunk too much Tio Pepe; it was unusual for her to force herself on others but then, she thought, it is a party and one circulates at parties. Beatrice was saying, 'Flora was suggesting I go abroad for the winter. We were discussing possibilities, such as Kenya. I've always wanted to see big game. Have you been on safari, Melinda?'

Although taken aback, Miss Pink forced herself to concentrate. 'Not as such. I've seen puma and grizzlies in the States, of course. Why don't you go? It would be just the thing; get away from this awful climate.'

'Distance myself from the climate of violence?' Beatrice suggested.

'That too. But why not? You have no pets, and the garden can take care of itself at this time of year. Kenya's relatively cheap.'

'There speaks the career woman! Flora takes the same view – and that's the heiress talking. Oh yes, you are, my dear' – as the girl shifted impatiently – 'Do you know the cost of a safari, Melinda? Two thousand pounds! I've made enquiries.'

'Sell something,' Miss Pink suggested.

Beatrice looked at her sternly and Flora said, 'Lateral thinking's the answer. Consider the situation from a different angle.'

157

'Such as?' Beatrice asked with interest.

'Look at it this way: the Highlands are uncongenial at this time of year.' She grinned. 'Right now they're actually unsafe, particularly for people on their own.'

'Your contemporaries call that going over the top.'

'I'm only thinking of your welfare.'

'I'm sure you are.' Beatrice patted the girl's hand. She looked at Miss Pink. 'Two thousand pounds isn't a lot to raise when you consider all your options,' she admitted. 'Would you come with me?'

Flora stood up. 'Mum's making signals. I'm probably needed in the kitchen. We'll get rid of the fuzz and then we'll eat.'

'Fuzz,' Beatrice repeated when she'd gone. 'How do they think of these words?'

Pagan, noticing movement on the part of his hosts, collected Anne and Esme and left, his flock under his wing. Behind him a flash of hysterical amusement subsided and during the subsequent meal people played raggedly with the new hypotheses – the significance of the streaker, Hamish's homosexuality – and allowed them to drop. Dinner was a subdued affair and the evening was not protracted. After coffee in the drawing room, the guests pleaded fatigue and took their leave.

'I'm falling asleep,' Beatrice said, collapsing in the car.

Miss Pink, recognising that this was not the moment for serious matters, made light conversation. 'We must talk about Kenya tomorrow. Are there other countries one might consider – less commercialised perhaps?'

'Possibly.'

'Why the sudden interest in badgers? Surely there must be a dozen species claiming precedence in Africa?'

'Who's interested in badgers?'

'Why, you. You were talking to Flora about them.'

After a few moments Beatrice asked, 'Is your hearing quite all it should be?'

'I have excellent hearing.' There was a pause. 'The hearing in one ear is slightly inferior to the other.'

'So is mine. It's not always easy to locate sound. You heard someone make a remark and it seemed to come from me.'

Miss Pink drove to Feartag, but declined the offer of a nightcap. They were both exhausted. A good night's sleep, they said, and they would meet in the morning. Beatrice promised to bolt her front door as soon as she was inside, and Miss Pink drove back to her little cottage, parked on the grass verge and went indoors.

She was so tired that she could hardly face the thought of reading in bed, but knew that if she didn't follow her nightly custom she would not unwind. Sighing heavily, she put a saucepan of milk on the stove and, ten minutes later, went upstairs with a cup of cocoa and the latest Tony Hillerman.

Usually she read a few pages while she drank the cocoa, and one more page afterwards. Then words started to blur, she would mark her place, remove the cardigan that protected her from the frosty air and put out the light.

Tonight was different. She had finished the cocoa and started on that last ritual page when, very distantly, she heard a familiar sound – although at first it was only the subconscious mind that was aware of it. The sound continued rhythmic, persistent, and she became aware of other factors – constriction, cold, a flood of light. She opened her eyes resentfully. The bedside light glared and she was lolling sideways on her pillows, still wearing her cardigan, Hillerman open on the quilt. Downstairs the telephone was ringing; it was one o'clock.

She went down the stairs carefully, knowing the dangers of haste in the small hours. She lifted the phone.

'Melinda? It's Beatrice. Can you come? I've shot him. The intruder. I heard him downstairs and I came down and – it must have been the glass I heard – he broke it: the glass pane in the french window – you know those windows—'

'Is he dead?' Miss Pink asked roughly.

'Oh. Oh, I hope not. I don't like to go near—'

'Stay there. If he moves, shoot him in the legs. I'll be with you in a moment.'

She grabbed her car keys and, in dressing gown and slippers, drove like a fury to Feartag, pulling up with a long skid on the gravel before the front door. Beatrice was on the step, holding a rifle.

159

'He hasn't moved,' she said. 'He's in the sitting room.'

Miss Pink took the rifle and went along the passage. The lights were on in the sitting room; one french window was open and sprawled on its face on the floor was a dark figure.

Miss Pink dropped to her knees and felt for a pulse in the neck. 'Help me get this thing off his head; it must be interfering with his breathing, if he's alive. No, don't turn him on his back, just free—' She stopped talking. They had peeled the black ski mask over the head and Flora's blank eyes stared along the jewelled carpet.

Chapter 15

'How could the girl be so *silly* – on this night of all nights?' The question was not rhetorical; across the kitchen table Beatrice pleaded for an answer. Miss Pink looked away: at the window, the stove, the brandy bottle between them. 'Everyone knew about Robert's guns,' Beatrice persisted. 'What could have possessed her?'

'Death wish?' hazarded Miss Pink. 'A compulsion towards self-destruction, or just a craving for high risks?'

'She was always taking risks.'

'The guns made it supremely exciting.'

'She didn't come here *because* I had the guns.'

'Pagan is going to ask why—' There was a pounding at the front door. 'Talk of the devil—' She left Beatrice and admitted the police herself. She gestured to the sitting room. 'It's there.'

'Where's Miss Swan?' Pagan asked.

'In the kitchen.'

He went along the passage, followed by Steer. She rejoined Beatrice. 'Have you any idea why Flora should come here?' she asked.

'None.' It was curt, as if Beatrice refused to consider a motive. She went on, 'Masked too, and gloved. Did you see those great thick gloves?'

'For breaking windows.'

Beatrice stared at the table. 'Unsuitable for autumn wear.'

Miss Pink said sharply, 'I'll put the kettle on again. There'll be a run on your tea and coffee tonight – this morning rather. I'd go back to bed if I were you, after Pagan has spoken to us. I'll stay, of course.'

'Are you suggesting I'd be able to sleep?'

'The body's at rest even if it's only lying down.' She winced at her own unfortunate wording.

161

Pagan loomed in the doorway, Steer behind him. 'Good morning, ma'am.'

'Morning?' Beatrice repeated stupidly.

'A nasty shock for you.' He looked at Miss Pink, who asked them to sit down. They pulled out chairs and all sat at the scrubbed wooden table like actors in a Christie play: the ladies in their warm dressing-gowns, Steer correctly dressed except for the absence of a tie, Pagan with his pyjama sleeves showing below the cuffs of his jacket.

'Did you move the body?' he asked.

'Only to get the mask off,' Miss Pink told him, 'and to free the airway. I wasn't sure, you see. . . . I'd already seen the exit wound – *a* wound, I mean, in the back – no, a tear – but even with the dark anorak there was so much blood . . .' She was gabbling.

'Quite.' Pagan turned back to Beatrice. 'Do you feel up to telling us what happened?' he asked gently.

After a while she said, 'I never thought I'd have to use it, you know. I locked and bolted everywhere so carefully, and then I thought how ridiculous all these precautions were; he had only to break a window and one would be at his mercy, as they say. I realised that I was totally helpless; that we all were – except yourselves. Presumably you're armed? You'd told us to stay indoors, bolt the doors, secure the windows, but you knew all along that there wasn't any security for us. I was very angry.' She looked at him steadily, then at Steer. No one was taking notes.

'I can see why you'd be angry, ma'am,' Pagan said.

'It would never have happened when my brother was alive,' Beatrice continued. 'I asked myself what he would have done – although no one would have dared to approach this house knowing Robert was inside. A man of great courage, Inspector; he was the Arctic explorer, Robert Swan. I'm sorry, I'm rambling. My brother would have slept with a loaded gun beside him, as he did abroad when dangerous predators were about. So I loaded his Winchester and put it by my bed. That made me feel much more secure.'

'It would,' Pagan said. 'What time would that be?'

'When?'

162

'When you went to bed.'

'The first time was shortly after Miss Pink brought me home, and that would have been about ten o'clock. But I couldn't sleep and it must have been about half an hour later that I got up and unlocked the gun cabinet. Even then it wasn't easy to get to sleep, but I must have done so eventually because I was wakened by something – I don't know what – and I was wide awake immediately. After a while, I picked up the rifle and went to the top of the stairs. I stayed there, listening, but I couldn't hear anything. All the windows were closed, so the river was scarcely audible. Then I heard the glass break – quite loud really. The noise came from the sitting room. Suddenly I was angry again. I didn't think of myself, only that this monster – as I thought – was about to destroy *my* property. For some reason, I thought of petrol bombs. I was quite convinced that a bottle had been thrown into the sitting room, or would be thrown through the broken window.' She made a helpless gesture. 'Old people get very attached to their possessions, Inspector, more so than they are to their own bodies perhaps. So I came downstairs in a rage, prepared to shoot as soon as I saw him. By the time I reached the sitting room he was inside and silhouetted against the glow of the street light. There's one on the bridge; it's only a faint glow but my eyes were accustomed to the dark by then. I fired straight at him. Had I thought about it, I might have aimed for the legs, but you don't think in a situation like that. I'd heard the glass break and here was the person responsible. And there was a murderer in the village.' She spread her hands. 'That's all.' Suddenly her face changed, became fiercely intense. 'But why Flora?' she demanded. 'Why?'

'There has to be a connection between her and Hamish,' Miss Pink said.

Six hours later, Feartag was in a quiet state of siege. While Beatrice and Miss Pink slept, or at least retired to rooms upstairs, various authorities had dealt with the body, finally removing it along with the carpet. The Press had been chivvied away from the drive, the gates closed and Knox stationed outside them in a police car guarding the property while he himself was in clear view of most people in the street, including other police officers. Miss Pink had discovered his presence when she got up to make a pot of coffee and glimpsed the car on the other side of the gates. From her angle, it looked as if it were blocking the exit from Feartag as much as protecting the occupants from curiosity seekers.

They breakfasted in the kitchen, but it wasn't until Beatrice was on her second cup of coffee and Miss Pink had assured her that, except for the missing window pane, all evidence of the night's events had been removed – not until then did she refer to the most astonishing aspect: a criminal connection between Flora and Hamish.

'They dressed similarly,' Beatrice agreed. 'At least when they broke into houses. What else is there to prove a connection?'

'There's not much proof of anything in this business,' Miss Pink said with unwonted vehemence. She had been thinking that there had been three violent deaths and the only one where the killer was known had been an accident. 'There were connections,' she went on. 'Hamish's telephone call to Flora – and since last night, I suspect that the reason for that call was much more important than to ask her for money.'

'He made it after he burned down Campbell's cottage.'

'And what effect would that information have on her? It would depend on why he set fire to the place. Was it to destroy his prints or to destroy Campbell? He – or they – wanted Campbell dead, because he was killed the following night. Why wasn't he killed the same night?'

'Because Hamish wasn't strong enough to kill a grown man.'

'What made him stronger the second night?'

'He'd acquired a gun then. His father has a shot-gun.'

'Campbell wasn't shot.'

'You can use the threat of a gun to control a victim while you engineer his murder in some other way, a way that can't be traced back to you.'

Miss Pink shook her head. 'That's impractical. If a lad is holding a gun on an adult, he keeps his distance. You need another . . . that's it! Another person. Flora came back and they killed Campbell between them.'

'She was in Edinburgh.' The tone was dull; Beatrice was beyond shock. 'You brought her home two days later.'

'She could drive, she could have borrowed a car. Let's work it out. We need a road atlas.'

The distance between Sgoradale and Edinburgh was 250 miles. 'Six hours at the very least,' Miss Pink said. 'She wouldn't risk going fast for fear of attracting attention from the police. She could drive here in the afternoon and evening, leave the car on a peat track out on the Lamentation Road, meet Hamish and they'd kill Campbell at the cove. She'd have time to get back to Edinburgh before dawn, and if she'd made the right excuse to her hosts no one need know she'd ever been away.'

'The owner of the car would find it had done 500 miles overnight.'

'She stole it and replaced it close to where she'd taken it from. If the owner had reported its loss, he might be so pleased to have it back undamaged he might not bother to mention to the police it had been taken for such a long joy-ride. And if he did, who'd connect that with a murder in the northern Highlands?'

'How would she steal it?'

'The thief operating in the car park here had keys; Pagan didn't mention finding keys in Hamish's room, but Flora could have kept them for him. I doubt if she stole from cars; the practice seems a trifle tame for her.'

'Tame?'

'Juvenile, I mean. Not much risk attached.'

'Mm. Yes.' Beatrice seemed to be following a line of her own.

Miss Pink said, 'When you suggested Hamish was homosexual, were you implying the boy was soliciting back in the summer?'

'What explanation do you have for the naked man not reporting the loss of his clothes – and car keys?'

'I wonder what happened to that man. Could he be traced? He had to repair his window. What kind of car did he have?

Who'd be likely to know that?'

'There was the man who saw him trying to get into his car – the one who spread the story around. He was in the hotel.'

'So he was.' Miss Pink lapsed into silence. 'And it would get you off the hook,' she murmured.

'I'm on the hook?' Beatrice asked politely.

'Pagan isn't interested in motivation; he wants to know who delivered the final blows to Campbell and Hamish, and where the boy's body was kept for two days. The rest is surmise so far, the product of what he'd call a hyperactive imagination. Apart from the nudist, I think the clue to the mystery lies in Flora's activities. I think she came here to kill you last night, probably in the same way that she killed Hamish – with a pillow over his mouth—'

'The person who did that got Hamish drunk and hit him with a piece of wood first.'

'Or they were drinking, and they quarrelled and she hit him.' Miss Pink thought for a moment and came to a decision. 'I'm going to Edinburgh. Will you be all right on your own?'

'With the police on the gate, yes. And the naked man?'

Miss Pink stood up. 'I'll see Butchart and find out if he can remember where that other man was staying. Since both men probably lived south of here, I may be able to kill several birds with one stone. What was the name of the barrister whom Flora was staying with?'

'Neil Fleming. Just a moment . . . ' as Miss Pink headed for the door. 'Did Flora repeat that 500-mile drive the following night in order to kill Hamish?'

Miss Pink halted, her lips pursed, then her face cleared. 'She didn't go back to Edinburgh. She stayed on, holed up somewhere – in an empty cottage perhaps. She returned to Edinburgh on the Sunday night, after killing Hamish.'

'Having concealed the body somewhere.'

'Ye-es.'

'And you brought her home on Tuesday, and she found some way to put the body in the sea on Tuesday night. You could do with some help in tracing her movements. Shall I come with you?'

'No. You've had enough excitement. And I have contacts, fixed points to start with. They'll lead to others.'

'I remember that fellow,' Butchart said. 'Ice in his whisky and complaints about my barman putting his cigarette in the ashtray while he was serving. Then he asked for the menu – and who was the chef? Then he said he'd decided he could make it for dinner at his own hotel, after all. Yes, I remember that customer!'

Miss Pink smiled in sympathy. 'And which hotel did he think was superior to this one?'

'He was staying at the Claymore in Morvern. Their chef can only do something called country cooking.'

'Was he well-known?'

'Who?'

'The photographer. The man who stayed at the Claymore.'

'I didn't know – oh, yes, he was sitting in his car changing a film, wasn't he? I don't remember that he mentioned his name.'

'He was called Osgood,' Alec said, tightening the pup's leash to prevent his jumping up at Miss Pink. 'I didn't meet him, but my dad did. He was staying at the Claymore and the date was August 4th.'

'How on earth do you remember that?'

'I went to the car park next day, to see if it was true, and I saw the broken glass on the ground. It wasn't like ordinary glass; a car window breaks into bits like tiny gravel.' He stopped and Miss Pink waited, her eyebrows raised. 'She hurt her paw,' he muttered, refusing to speak the poodle's name, 'and I remember dates when they had to do with her. I thought she got a bit of glass between the pads, but she was better next day.'

The receptionist at the Claymore wanted to play it by the rules. 'Shouldn't you tell me why you want to know?' she asked.

'He's a photographer,' Miss Pink explained. 'I allowed him to take a picture of my house on condition he sent me a copy. He did and it's quite exquisite. I want Christmas cards made from it. The trouble is copyright, you know? He stamped the back of

167

the print with his name and phone number, but I can't get any reply. It must be an old stamp.'

The receptionist was turning back the pages of the register. 'August 4th, you said? Here it is: Hedley Osgood, Aberdeen. That doesn't help you much.'

Miss Pink thanked her effusively and drove south. It was six o'clock before she managed to get Hedley Osgood on the end of a telephone line. The number Directory Enquiries had given her was for his home address and she'd tried it three times, shivering in desolate call-boxes on the open road. Finally she booked a room in the Caledonian at Inverness, not wanting to go further until she had spoken to Osgood. When she did reach him he was off-hand at first, but intimidated as soon as she adopted an exaggerated air of authority. Her voice, naturally deep, could pass for a man's when she chose. She was, she told him, a detective inspector involved in the Sgoradale murders. He was amazed to find that his own odd experience could interest the police, but he agreed to meet her the following lunch-time. There was a pause while she pretended to note down the address of a city bar. 'One other thing,' she said before ringing off, 'What kind of car was he driving?'

'A VW Golf. White.'

'Why do you remember it so well?'

'I took a picture. It's pinned up over my desk. I'm a supermarket manager.'

'You didn't happen to get the registration number?'

'No. I can let you have a print though.'

'I'd be obliged.' She rang off. He might contact Pagan when the mythical detective inspector failed to materialise in Aberdeen, but she wasn't bothered. By that time Pagan should have more important things to think about.

The yellow pages gave her the Volkswagen garages in the area and by mid-morning next day she had the information she needed. This time she posed as an insurance agent, but it was the confidence of her bearing as much as the bogus occupation which persuaded the manager of the relevant garage to produce his records. She was in luck; the motorist with the smashed window had paid his bill by cheque and the office had his

address: 'We always ask for it in the case of a cheque.' The
driver's name was J. P. Geddes and he had given an address in
Stirling.

Montrose Gardens was a fairly new estate on the outskirts of
Stirling and No. 16 was what agents refer to as 'ranch style'. A
picture window gave a bleak view of a room that extended the
depth of the house to another wall that was mostly glass. The
room was sparsely furnished in grey and pale yellow, with a lot
of bare shelves and a music centre. There was a light over the
doorbell but no one came to Miss Pink's ring. After some
minutes a woman in her thirties came out of a house opposite
and crossed the road.

'Are you looking for Mr Geddes? Can I help you?'

Miss Pink looked confused. 'Not Geddes. Jameson – Mr and
Mrs Jameson. She's my niece.'

'You must have the wrong address. Have you got it written
down anywhere?'

'I have it committed to memory. 16 Montrose Gardens.'

'That's the address, but Mr Geddes lives here and he's not
married. He's all on his own.'

'Geddes,' Miss Pink repeated. 'It doesn't even sound like
Jameson.'

'And your niece is married, so you're looking – hold on! Are
you all right?'

Miss Pink's eyelids drooped as she swayed on her feet. 'Just a
little dizzy,' she breathed. 'I'm not as young as I was.'

'Look, come into my house and let me make you a cup of
tea.'

She was helped across the road and into another bleak living
room, this one in beige. Beyond the window No. 16 returned
her stare enigmatically. When the tea was brought she had a
story ready about being homeward bound to Berwick from a
visit to an old friend in Dingwall. Her hostess's name was
Jefferies and she was good-hearted but not over-intelligent.
Miss Pink invented a brother in Falkirk who would disentangle
the mistake in the address, then she looked back at No. 16.
'Who lived there before him?' she asked.

'Now that I don't know. We've only been here eighteen months and he's been in that house at least three years. He bought it when he started at Earl's Hill – that's the local school; John is a schoolmaster. But wouldn't you have known if your niece left Montrose Gardens three years ago?'

Miss Pink looked embarrassed. 'She could have given me her new address and I remembered the old one. You know how it is.'

'Never mind. Have another tea-cake.'

Miss Pink ate greedily as old people do, mesmerised by the huge window. 'So sad,' she said. 'A young man living alone.'

Mrs Jefferies smiled indulgently. 'He has interests – hiking and mountain climbing, and he takes kids on trips. This weekend he's youth hostelling in the Trossachs with a group and he won't be back until Sunday night.' Miss Pink listened with polite interest, visibly recovering her energy with the tea.

She drove away hoping that the woman didn't have the wit to wonder why her doddery old visitor should own a sporty Renault GTL. The last thing she wanted was for Geddes to come home to the news that someone was making enquiries about him. What had terrified the man two months ago might have even more power to terrify him now.

Neil Fleming, the barrister, lived in a Georgian terrace north of Princes Street in Edinburgh. The door was answered by a middle-aged person who showed Miss Pink into an airy room overlooking a walled garden. After a few minutes an attractive woman entered. She was a slim blonde and, like Coline MacKay, looked far too young to have a grown daughter.

'I'm Sidonie Fleming,' she said, none too warmly. 'Did you have an appointment with my husband?'

'Perhaps you can help me,' Miss Pink said. 'It's about Flora MacKenzie. I'm from Sgoradale.'

The woman caught her breath and her eyes blazed. '*Coline* sent you?'

'No one sent me,' Miss Pink said quietly.

Mrs Fleming made an obvious effort to pull herself to-gether, nevertheless her response was menacing. 'You've

170

come on behalf of the MacKenzie girl?'

'I'm a friend of Beatrice Swan, the old lady who shot Flora. My name is Melinda Pink.'

'Ah, that could make a difference. And Coline MacKay doesn't know you've come to see me? So why did you?'

'Neither Coline nor anyone else had any idea of what was going on. Flora appeared to be a healthy captivating girl, a little young for her age perhaps—'

Mrs Fleming gave a sardonic laugh, but her eyes were furious. 'Captivating is not the word I'd have chosen. Flora was a slut, and the only thing that surprises me is that she was shot by accident. If I'd been here, I'd have strangled her with my bare hands.'

'Why did you invite her here?' Miss Pink was the picture of innocence.

'*I didn't!* I was in the Seychelles and she invited herself in my absence. I'd never have left two young girls alone in this house without adequate supervision. I'd be thinking in terms of *loco parentis*, my God – and I'd have been a world away from the reality of the situation. You think I'm exaggerating; you imagine she just – what? Made a pass at my husband? Held all-night parties in the house with hard drugs? All right, you haven't come from Coline but when you go back to Sgoradale, you can tell her about what I'm going to show you. Unless you see it you won't believe it. I didn't; my daughter had to show me.'

Miss Pink was driven to another Georgian terrace, to a house that was less immaculate than the one she'd left and where the hall and lift held an air of seedy transience. They rode to the third floor and Mrs Fleming produced a key which opened the door of a large room. Inside was a double bed, a dressing table and easy chairs either side of an old-fashioned gas-fire. There was a glass ash-tray on a bedside table, under a lamp with a dingy shade. On the dressing-table were a bottle of whisky half-full, one of gin unopened, and several bottles of tonic water and bitter lemon.

The room's proportions had been spoiled by a partition that boxed off one corner. A flimsy door was open to show a

171

bathroom, some towels, a tablet of soap and a toothbrush.

'Utilitarian,' Miss Pink murmured. 'Not a joyful place. Who pays the rent?'

'The keyholder was an F. MacMasters but there's no such person. The rent was paid by my daughter and Flora MacKenzie, in advance, which is how I come to have the key. I got it from my daughter and I was waiting for Flora to come back and claim it.'

'What would you have done then?' Miss Pink asked, opening a wardrobe.

'I hadn't thought. I was looking forward to it actually. Maybe your friend's saved me from a murder charge.'

'I see your point.' Miss Pink was shifting clothes along a rail: a mini-skirt and long jacket in thin red leather, a jumpsuit in black lace, a kind of mock trench-coat in a dark silky fabric. There was a similar fur to the one which Flora had been wearing when she was picked up at Buffy MacLean's: long-haired, but this was white. On the floor of the wardrobe were shoes with very high heels or huge platform soles. 'It's sad rather than depressing,' Miss Pink said. 'One wonders why they had to do it.'

Mrs Fleming answered promptly. 'Flora needed the money; she was an heiress, but Coline kept her on a very short rein. But basically, she did this for kicks. She wasn't into drugs or drink; she took care of her body.' A spasm contorted the woman's face. 'There are condoms in the bedside table. Can you believe that? A sixteen-year-old tart frightened of Aids. Not many have been used. According to Charlotte, my daughter, Flora quickly got bored with this' – she gestured at the room – 'and said there were easier and safer ways to make money. They're supposed to have used this place only a few times. And now you're wondering why my daughter did it. Well, it was partly because Flora is . . . was the stronger character, but mostly because she's evil: seductive in every sense of the word. She made mincemeat of my husband. And shall I tell you why she had to seduce him? Of course he wasn't interested in her, he's a workaholic anyway, but he was a challenge to her and she broke him down. But she got more than she bargained for. She'd be

172

used to married men keeping quiet, but Neil had to tell me: no way was he going to let Charlotte see her again. He said he'd never met anyone so corrupt – and he's a criminal lawyer. And he didn't know about this place.'

Mrs Fleming lit a cigarette with a gold lighter, pacing the room like a dog, stiff with hatred. She went on, 'It was through my husband that I was able to get the truth out of Charlotte. The girls had spent hours away from the house and it was essential to me that I found out what they'd been doing. When I told Charlotte that her friend had been in bed with her father, she told me everything. They used to pick up men in bars. In good hotels they wore long coats over those ridiculous clothes. Those in the wardrobe are Flora's; Charlotte's were thrown in a skip.'

'How can I find out where Flora was on Saturday and Sunday of last weekend?'

'Why do you want to know?'

'You knew Flora was dead. Don't you know of the other events in Sgoradale?'

Mrs Fleming was still, the only movement the smoke from her cigarette. 'There have been two other deaths: the policeman's son and the MacKays' handyman. They had something to do with Flora? Why should I be surprised? She was capable of anything.'

'Those two nights,' Miss Pink pressed.

'Let's go home. Charlotte should be back from school. She's very subdued; I've put the fear of death into her – and that's a remark in bad taste if ever there was one.'

Charlotte Fleming was a pretty and very frightened girl. Under her mother's eye she agreed to tell Miss Pink what she could remember of Flora's movements, but even the first question was unwelcome. When asked where Flora had been the previous Saturday evening, her mouth opened and closed and her eyes were anguished.

'You can't do her any harm now,' Miss Pink said. 'Promises are annulled by death.'

'She never asked me to promise.' The girl picked at the piping on the sofa. 'She spent the night at the flat.'

'Did you see her there?'

'No.'

'So how do you know that's where she was?'

'Because she told me.'

'When did she go to the flat?'

'Saturday afternoon. About three o'clock.'

'And when did you see her again?'

'Breakfast time – about eight o'clock.'

'She came down for breakfast at eight on Sunday? And when did she go away again?'

'Monday evening.'

'*Monday?* Where was she on Sunday?'

'With me.'

'Are you quite—'

Mrs Fleming interrupted sharply. 'You want to find out where Flora was on Sunday? Or where she wasn't?'

'I need to know if she could have been in Sgoradale between Sunday breakfast time and Tuesday morning.'

'How much time did she spend with you on Sunday?' Mrs Fleming asked her daughter. 'There's no need to say what you were doing – just where, and was she with you?'

Charlotte looked at her shoe. 'We were at the flat or . . . or together until Sunday evening. Then Daddy took us to the Rendezvous.'

'They came straight home from the restaurant.' Mrs Fleming held Miss Pink's eye. 'That is, the girls split up. Flora returned to this house, Charlotte went to visit a friend.' Miss Pink said nothing. 'Go and help Jeannie with the tea,' Mrs Fleming told the girl. She turned back as the footsteps receded. 'Flora was with my husband until late that evening,' she said bitterly. 'And Charlotte had gone to that ghastly place to meet – oh, let's forget why she ever went there, can we? Anyway, she came home some time after midnight and looked in on Flora, who was in her own bed – for a change. So she couldn't have been in Sgoradale. Charlotte can fill you in on the rest.'

'It's possible that, in telling me this, you won't have to talk to the police.'

'And you'll keep it to yourself – the details, I mean; you'll

174

consider my family, not to speak of my husband's career?'

'I'm also considering Coline and Ranald.'

'God! Those poor things. How was Coline to know?'

'And I want to clear Beatrice Swan.'

'How can you? She shot the girl.'

'If Flora can be shown to be responsible for the two murders, Beatrice is in the position of a householder defending herself against a killer who almost certainly intended to kill her. She'll have everyone's sympathy.'

'She must have a good deal of that now.'

'There's an element of public opinion that disapproves of people defending themselves with firearms.'

Charlotte and the housekeeper came in with afternoon tea. When the woman had left, Miss Pink returned to her questions, obstructed by a mother determined that her daughter should not say in as many words that she'd been dabbling in prostitution. Despite this, and the emotional state of mother and daughter, it seemed that Flora couldn't have left Edinburgh between Sunday breakfast time and Monday evening, when the girls met Buffy MacLean in the bar of the North British Hotel and Flora asked him for a lift to Slaggan. 'Lady MacKay called on Monday and told her she'd got to go home,' Charlotte explained.

'And you had to go back to school,' her mother said meaningly. 'And I was due back from the Seychelles. So when was the boy killed? Sunday night, I take it.'

Miss Pink looked at Charlotte's blank face and shook her head. The mother was more concerned with her hatred for the dead girl than the state of mind of the living one. She sipped her tea and wondered how Flora had engineered Hamish's death.

There was still an hour of daylight remaining when she left the Fleming house and the weather was fine. This was Friday and if she were to wait until Geddes returned to Stirling on Sunday night, she was faced with the daunting prospect of a weekend of idleness. On the other hand, the Trossachs were only fifty miles away and she should have no difficulty in locating Geddes. The atlas showed only two youth hostels in the area.

She struck lucky at the first attempt: a mini-bus from Earl's Hill School was obvious among the vehicles outside the hostel. This was a Victorian country house, brilliantly lit and packed with youngsters. She felt a surge of confidence; the journey had been uneventful and, in order to give her quarry time to get supper out of the way, she had stopped in Callendar for a meal. Fresh and alert, she emerged from the Renault, smoothed her skirt and advanced on the youth hostel.

A girl with spiky hair took her to Geddes, who was supervising washing-up: a gangling man in his late thirties with a large nose, thinning hair and worried eyes. He regarded Miss Pink with an astonishment that was quickly suppressed, but not before she had seen the alarm in his eyes. She retreated to the empty hall and he followed. 'What is it?' he asked and then, carefully, 'What can I do for you? Have we met?'

'My name is Pink.' She gave him an old card, one with JP after her name. He turned pale. 'Shall we sit in my car?' she suggested. 'It's a pleasant evening.'

'Do you mind telling me what this is about?' he asked stiffly as the doors closed on the outside world.

'Does the name Flora MacKenzie mean anything to you?'

'I . . . don't think so. I've taught a lot of children.'

'Or Hamish Knox?'

She was turned towards him and he must have been aware of her scrutiny, but he made no attempt to speak. The silence stretched agonisingly. At length she broke it. 'You weren't the only victim.'

He looked at her then, but in the refracted light neither could read the other's expression. 'I wasn't?' he breathed and, in the same dull tone, 'I haven't the remotest idea what you're talking about.'

'The girl was called Flora MacKenzie.'

'What girl?'

'You were photographed as you were trying to get into your car.'

After another silence he gave a small sigh. 'So that card was a hoax. Clever though; you look just like a JP.'

'I was a JP.'

'What happened? Were you de-frocked when they found out you were blackmailing poor sods who'd been up in front of you on the bench?'

'How much blackmail have you paid to date?'

'Who's talking about me being blackmailed?'

'You're terrified of it. I'm legitimate and I'm here to try to find the explanation for two murders. They were associated with your experience in Sgoradale, and both victims were killed because they knew too much. If they'd shared their information, they wouldn't have been killed. Were those children blackmailing you?'

He didn't respond immediately, but stared into the night. After a time he sighed again and said, 'No. Yes. Only in the first place, but I was terrified they'd come back. My life's been a torment for weeks. I haven't got the courage to kill myself, but I did consider . . . I thought about killing them. No, they're not blackmailing me; I've got nothing they can take.'

'You have a nice house.'

'You know about that? I suppose you know everything about me. Those two didn't want money; they took over a hundred pounds off me, but that was just for laughs. The object of the exercise was straight viciousness. They'd beaten an adult, a teacher. Authority, right? It was a put-up job; I worked that out eventually. That boy didn't come on us by accident when he was out shooting rabbits; he was waiting for her to bring me to a place that they probably used over and over again with any other poor sucker she could entice into the woods – and who'd believe my story? I was trapped. God, I was glad when he got himself murdered, and I know exactly how he felt – the guy who did it. There but for the grace of God . . . '

'It seems that Flora killed him, and you postulate a motive. His nerve cracked and she had to silence him.'

He shook his head. 'She got someone to do it for her then. A child of twelve hasn't the strength to kill a boy of sixteen. She's only a little thing.'

'How did you allow yourself to be seduced by a twelve-year-old, however charming?'

'She said she was seventeen, she looked seventeen—'

177

'She looked twelve,' Miss Pink said firmly.

'Jesus!' He slumped in his seat. 'You've got no proof, not even of this conversation. It's not taking place; no one knows.'

'Exactly. So tell me how they managed to relieve you of your possessions.'

'I said – he had a gun. Didn't they use a gun on the other victims?'

'They had different methods, but a gun was used on one person – not to kill him, but as a threat.'

'I saw through it eventually,' he repeated savagely. 'I've had nothing else to think about for weeks. She's a better actor than him. She really did appear to be frightened of him. He can't be her brother – different names, I suppose he's her half-brother – it's immaterial. And then, he saying he'd fetch his father and she saying he'd keep quiet if I gave him money. So I gave him everything I had and he was laughing. He was standing on my clothes and when he told me to run and lifted the gun, I ran. But I swear to you she told me she was seventeen.'

'She was sixteen.'

'But you said – *he* said she was *twelve*! His kid sister, he said: twelve years old.'

Chapter 16

'So that was the game: pick a victim, entice him into the woods, big brother turns up – after rabbits with a shot-gun – and tells the victim his sister is twelve years old. Child molestation; it's a variation on the badger game.'

Miss Pink was home again, back in the sitting room at Feartag. A new carpet had been laid and the pane of glass replaced in the french window. 'It's good to be here,' she said, looking round the room.

'It's good to have you back,' Beatrice responded. 'When do you propose to tell Pagan about this terrible double life of Flora's?'

Miss Pink didn't answer directly. She said, 'I can see how Campbell's murder was worked, but if Flora were alive she'd have an alibi for that night – probably a client in the Edinburgh flat, and it would be up to the police to prove he didn't exist. On the other hand, they might unearth a record of a car stolen in Edinburgh that night, which reappeared later with five hundred extra miles on the clock. All the same, those records would be complicated if Flora left the car in a poor part of the city with the keys in the ignition, and it was then stolen by a petty thief.'

'But there would be a record, even if the car was stolen twice.'

'And the police are good on these meticulous time-consuming enquiries.' But Miss Pink did not sound convinced.

'What is the rest of the case against her?'

'Them. They were in it together. The evidence is circumstantial – and how unusual is that? Campbell saw something, knew something – suspected the worst, being Campbell. I doubt that he was aware of the seriousness of his position until near the end . . .'

'He came to me for a gun; if I'd let him have one, he could still be alive.'

'We're not responsible for other people. You thought he was paranoid, or playing a game. No one knew whether he was harmless or dangerous, but Hamish knew that Campbell could expose them – or thought he could – so he set fire to the cottage and then panicked – or his panic increased – and he sent for Flora, phoning her from Camas Beag. She came and destroyed the people who could expose her, first one then the other.'

'Could they have sent Campbell an anonymous letter?'

'No, his reactions were too unpredictable. In any case, they sent only one: to Esme. She was a sitting duck – as you were in a different context: the elderly lady deprived of the protection of a strong man. No wonder you got nasty telephone calls.'

'You're saying the only motive was to terrorise people.'

'You need more? It's adequate for all anonymous callers, heavy breathers. There's a sense of power, a flouting of authority, thrills: heady stuff. Geddes understands: "It's how they get their kicks," he said. Hamish wasn't so bad; he followed, she led – and no man can be as vicious as a woman.'

'She wasn't a woman. So Hamish was killed because he was weak.'

'Because he was a threat. His nerve had broken, he forgot to wear gloves when he broke into Campbell's cottage to try to find out once and for all what the man knew. Flora wouldn't have allowed him to do that had she been here, but she'd gone off to Edinburgh after the altercation that I witnessed – when Hamish thundered away and rode down the poodle. With Flora gone, Hamish had lost his anchor, so he tried a spot of villainy on his own – to prove his value perhaps. Could I be right?' Beatrice looked blank. Miss Pink went off on another tack. 'But how did Flora kill the boy? She had alibis from Sunday breakfast time onwards, and Hamish was alive until late on Sunday night. Pagan might say she had the motive, so never mind the opportunity. Perhaps he'll close the case.'

'You said a moment ago she destroyed both of them.'

'She was responsible for their destruction. She meant to kill Hamish. She'd set him up as Campbell's killer. Campbell never returned to the island that night; they killed him on the shore and used his boat to reach the island. The fact that there were no prints on the dixies, the boat sunk in water that was too shallow – those weren't mistakes but pointers, first to foul play and then to the identity of the perpetrator. Hamish was the fall guy, and by the time the police got to him he would be dead: a faked suicide perhaps – by drowning. You look surprised.'

'I'm amazed – at how you've worked it all out. Why didn't she kill Hamish, then, immediately after they'd killed Campbell?'

'He ran away.'

'But he had his father's gun!'

'He'd never use it on her; he was terrified, but if he wasn't infatuated with her he was the only male that came within her orbit who wasn't. Flora used sex as a weapon, and Hamish was immature emotionally; he must have been in a fine turmoil – and that would bother her. Like Campbell, Hamish would have become unpredictable; like Campbell, he had to go. He ran too fast that night, and she had to get back to Edinburgh to sustain her alibi. She ran the risk of his talking before she could get back and kill him, but it wasn't much of a risk; they were now partners in murder.'

Miss Pink sighed and stood up. She crossed to the french windows and looked out at the bare birches. After a moment she undid the latch and stepped out on the terrace. Beatrice followed and they stood at the rail while the river talked busily below them.

'How much did his father suspect?' Miss Pink asked. 'He knew Hamish was responsible for the prank with the police car, but – more than that? At some point he locked his gun away. The night Hamish was killed, he was defenceless.'

'He was always defenceless.'

'Flora was going to return, so he had to find another gun; he was desperate: trying to equalise his position with a firearm. He entered a house with the intention of acquiring one. What I can't understand is how he was persuaded to drink. He was the violator; how did his victim turn the tables?'

Beatrice smiled. 'It's a neat technical problem. Could it have been a variation on the Stockholm syndrome, where a bond is formed between terrorists and hostages? Hamish could have

181

entered a house armed with some weapon – a knife, perhaps –
but instead of killing his victim he was persuaded to talk, and
then to drink. According to you he was confused: frightened of
Flora, yet obsessed by her, knowing he must kill her or she'd
kill him. He could have been aching to talk to someone and it
wouldn't matter; he meant to kill the person he was confiding
in anyway. He'd talk a lot, he'd get thirsty, he'd drink –
anything.'

'It's a reasonable hypothesis, but why was he suffocated after
he'd been hit on the head?'

'Because the first blow didn't kill him? And a second could
have resulted in blood on – what? The furnishings?'

'You're proposing one of his victims for the role of killer?'

'Their victims,' Beatrice corrected. 'But we don't know who
those were, do we? There could be any number of people who
kept quiet about victimisation. There could have been some
motive for killing him that hasn't crossed our minds. Self-
defence isn't good enough because, once he'd been knocked
unconscious, the police could have been sent for—'

'His own father?'

'Why not, if the boy was only unconscious? There is no
excuse; there was an intention to kill, and there was no
remorse. The body was concealed.'

Miss Pink turned and surveyed the back of the house: grey
stone laced with ivy except where a Virginia creeper flamed
around the door of the log cellar. 'He had to be kept close to
water,' she said. 'So Flora was never a double killer.'

Beatrice changed the emphasis. 'There's no *case* against her.
There's no proof, there isn't even circumstantial evidence, and
all those people you approached over the last two days are
going to deny everything. You obtained information by
methods the police couldn't use – and Geddes didn't even know
Flora was dead. If he had known, you wouldn't have got a word
out of him.'

'If Pagan suspected the truth, I wonder what he might do
about it.'

'There's a nip in the air; shall we go in?'

They returned to the sitting room and Beatrice closed the

182

french windows. 'You'll tell him what you discovered?'

'Of course. What I found out about Flora's activities doesn't exonerate you legally for her death, but morally you're in the clear, and she killed Campbell.'

'You don't sound convinced.'

'I know you'd never sleep with your window closed, so what kind of noise did you hear above the sound of the river that woke you and made you get up?'

'The river doesn't make much sound when the water's low.'

Miss Pink ignored this. 'And how did you get downstairs and into this room after she broke the glass? She'd have moved too fast. Either she'd have met you in the passage or she'd have hidden herself to wait for you to show up.'

'Pagan was satisfied with my statement.'

'You were waiting for her downstairs,' Miss Pink went on. 'The place was in darkness, the curtains drawn back, a faint glow through the windows from the light on the bridge. You'd have seen her approach the house and you'd picked on this room as the most likely point of entry.'

'You're making the assumption that I knew an intruder was going to come to my house.'

'That's what you might say to Pagan, and what policeman would believe that an old lady would use blackmail as a lure and herself as live bait? But Pagan didn't hear you mention a badger and two thousand pounds.'

'Nor did anyone else.'

They regarded each other without expression. Beatrice said, 'Before capital punishment was struck off the statute book, we delegated justice to a judge and a jury and the public executioner.'

'I've lived in states where capital punishment still exists.'

'I haven't forgotten. So you condoned it.'

'You can't blame legalised killing on me,' Miss Pink protested. 'I'm not responsible.'

'That's your choice,' Beatrice said equably. 'But someone has to be.'

Detroit City Ordinance 29-85, Section 29-2-2(b) provides: "Any person who retains any library material or any part thereof for more than fifty (50) calendar days beyond the due date shall be guilty of a misdemeanor."